HOT
STATE

HOT STATE

A Slightly Crooked Mystery

Perry Anthony

an imprint of

PROSPECTIVE PRESS LLC

1959 Peace Haven Rd, #246, Winston-Salem, NC 27106 U.S.A.
www.prospectivepress.com

Published in the United States of America by PROSPECTIVE PRESS LLC

HOT STATE
A SLIGHTLY CROOKED MYSTERY

Text copyright © Perry Anthony, 2019
All rights reserved.
The author's moral rights have been asserted.

Cover and interior design by ARTE RAVE

ISBN 978-1-943419-91-3

First PROSPECTIVE PRESS trade paperback edition

Printed in the United States of America
First printing November 2019

The text of this book is typeset in Marion
Accent text is typeset in Helvetica Neue

Space Oddity
Words and Music by David Bowie
© Copyright 1969 (Renewed) Onward Music Ltd., London, England
TRO-Essex Music International, Inc., New York, controls all publication rights for the U.S.A. and Canada
International Copyright Secured   Made in U.S.A.
All Rights Reserved Including Public Performance for Profit
Used by Permission

Theme From "The Monkees" (Hey, Hey We're The Monkees)
Words and Music by Tommy Boyce and Bobby Hart
Copyright © 1966 Sony/ATV Music Publishing LLC and Screen Gems-EMI Music Inc.
Copyright Renewed
All Rights Administered by Sony/ATV Music Publishing LLC, 424 Church Street, Suite 1200, Nashville, TN 37219
International Copyright Secured All Rights Reserved
Reprinted by Permission of Hal Leonard LLC

We'll Meet Again
Words and Music by Ross Parker and Hughie Charles
Copyright © 1939 (Renewed) Dash Music Company Limited
International Copyright Secured All Rights Reserved
Reprinted by Permission of Hal Leonard LLC

Cover element © Orchi. Used with permission.

HOT
STATE

One

It was a small, white building that seemed to want to hide from the world, set back deep from the boulevard, the space in between obfuscated by an overgrown oak whose roots were buckling the sidewalk. Damon Ramp drove by it twice trying to make a one o'clock appointment, but seventy years of nature and muddled urban renewal made him settle for a one-fifteen. Over the transom was a rusted, galvanized sign riveted into the glazed white brick, which simply read BARBERS. It was an old, two-chair shop, but somewhere along the way someone attached a brownstone addition, none too cleverly slapped on the back. Curiosity about the odd little building and its place in the uptown neighborhood's eclectic landscape of commercial and residential structures drew Damon in for a closer look. Mostly it was just plain wondering if he had the right address.

The address was right, embossed in arched gold lettering on each of the building's two picture windows. Below one of the twin 606s, crudely painted in a Gothic, midnight-blue script, was the new name: PETAL TO THE METAL. Damon chuckled at the name but came up empty when he tried to connect the Gothic, heavy metal connotation with one of his favorite things, flowers. He cupped his hands around his glasses to look inside, focusing in on a menu of wares the shop offered: BLACK ARTS SUPPLIES · BODY PIERCINGS & TATTOOS · LEATHERS · PALMIST · FETISH ROOM. Incidentally, at the bottom of the list, RARE FLOWERS. The classification given on his preprinted contract was simply "flowers." Perhaps a reclassification was in order. He stepped inside.

The mirrors from its barbershop days were still intact, perfectly aligned with the two shop windows. A long, glass display case filled with unrecognizable sundries stood in place of the barber chairs, which found new life in the corner anchoring the waiting area. To the right, under the glow of a red neon script that read DARK ROOM, was a large, heavily tattooed bald man in black leather pants and a matching vest, slouched in a wooden chair with his legs boldly spread, an adult magazine in front of his face. A red curtain played go-between with the man and whatever was in that back room. He didn't reveal his face. He revealed only one word, in a rough and husky voice: "Milah."

A pale, thirtyish woman with long, black hair came out from behind the curtain. She was wearing a thick, oversized black turtleneck over a long, brown corduroy skirt that hovered above a chunky pair of Doc Martens. Her eyes were dark and thick with mascara. She was holding a Chinese takeout box of what looked and smelled like pad Thai, with two chopsticks poking straight out of the top, like they were angrily shoved into the noodles after her lunch was so rudely interrupted.

"Dammit, Burl, put that thing away, you freak. Couldn't you look at a goddam *People* once in a while?" She backhanded the magazine, slapping it into his face. Burl kept on reading. "Hey—didja hear me?" She kicked one of his studded, buckled boots. "Hey, do something, wouldja?"

Burl made a slobbering, lapping sound, licking one of the pages from the bottom up, lifting the XXX mask that covered his goateed face. Bulky, silver hoops hung from his ears and nose.

"I'm having lunch, too," he said.

Milah gave up on Burl and approached Damon.

"You the phone company guy?"

"Hi, Milah. I'm Damon Ramp from *NewStar*." He pushed up his thick black glasses and held out his hand to greet her.

"Sorry, I get paid to do that," she said, refusing to shake his hand, motioning her head toward the menu of services. "Plus, you look a little pale. Stupid, disease-spreading convention if you ask me. I hate doing readings in the winter. I feel like dipping my hands in bleach every time I touch someone's hand."

"I take it you're the palmist then?" Damon asked.

"Yeah, that and babysitting the good-for-nothing freak over in the corner." She made sure Burl heard her. Burl kept on reading. "We do other things, too..."

"Look, I'm sorry to interrupt your lunch, but do you mind telling me a little about your business? How long have you been here?"

"I don't mind as long as you don't mind if I eat while I tell ya. I hate cold pad Thai—gets all dried out when you nuke it. Whaddaya want to know?"

"How long have you been in business?"

"Oh, about six months or so." She pushed some noodles into her mouth and chewed a few bites. "Cool old building—always reminded me of a White Castle. Gotta have those sliders once in a while, you know? You like gut bombs?"

"Sure, just never before midnight and a six-pack," Damon fibbed. He rarely drank anything stronger than iced tea. "That's quite a menu of services. I've got you listed as a flower shop, but it looks like you do a lot more than that. Do you have a specialty?"

Milah coyly shrugged. "Well...*specialties* about captures it. You have a classification for that?"

"Milah, we have a classification for just about anything you can think of. Just tell me what part of your business you want to grow, and we'll help you get there."

"Well, I like growing things," Milah said, slurping some more noodles. "That would be a cool classification. Yeah, just put us under—"

A young man burst through the front door, breathless and panicked. He rushed past Damon like he wasn't even there. "Milah, Milah, we need to talk," he struggled out between breaths. Milah held up her index finger to silence him. It did. It stopped him in his tracks, save for the rushed breaths and gasps coming from the clean-cut kid. He looked about sixteen, and his clothes didn't come cheap, J. Crew and Abercrombie probably, right down to his underwear. Milah gestured with her other hand toward Burl, who picked up where Milah left off, guiding him behind the curtain into the DARK ROOM. There was a strange mastery in the way she handled the situation. She'd done this before. And so had he.

"Sorry, gotta go," Milah said. "But if you come back again sometime with a bag of sliders, maybe I'll give you the tour—looks like you could use a little excitement."

Two

Damon's first call on Friday morning was a mom-and-pop drug-store right by the state Capitol. The shop had somehow managed to stay in business despite being surrounded by a pair of competing national chains—probably so entrenched in their own battle that they overlooked the little mouse hiding in the corner. Damon felt that twinge of brightness that Friday brings, a twinge further brightened by a peek of March sunshine, that first hint of spring, the warmest day in four months. He even started to feel downright lucky when he found a good place to park on Rice Street, with a nice fat opening cut into the snowbank so he wouldn't have to play Admiral Peary today. Small-scale climbing expeditions now awaited him before each call, due to a broken driver's side door handle that had snapped off the week before. Damon scooted across the seat to exit the passenger side, and stepped into the nice fat opening—and into a nice fat puddle of ankle-deep slush. Then he went back to feeling how he usually did. He cursed Pontiac again and went inside.

There was a sweet old man behind the counter, about Mickey Rooney height with a Mickey Rooney hairline, but with a pair of eyeglasses that screamed 1987, when just about everything was just too damned big. They were the eyeglasses equivalent to the giant cell phone Gordon Gekko used in *Wall Street*. World War I aviator goggles were smaller, and this guy looked old enough to maybe have a pair of those, too. And he was really, really happy—humming and whistling and doing a little soft-shoe behind the counter. The kind of bubbly happiness Mickey Rooney's Andy Hardy always had. If Judy Garland walked in they'd probably put on a show.

"Good morning," Damon said, stepping forward with a squish from his soggy foot. "I'm Damon Ramp from *NewStar*. Are you Harry?"

"Well I certainly am, Mr. Ramp," Harry said, bright as March sunshine. "A pleasure to meet you, sir. Harry Keillor."

Harry stepped forward and bowed, doing a theatrical loop-to-loop with his hand before extending it to Damon.

"Keillor?" Damon asked, shaking Harry's hand. "You're not related to the *Prairie Home Companion* Keillor, are you?"

"No relation whatsoever. A mean old bear, what I hear. Don't let that prairie charm fool you, yes indeedy. What can I do for you, Mr. Ramp?"

"We spoke on the phone about you doing some advertising in the yellow pages. You have an absolutely charming store, Mr. Keillor."

Behind the counter was a high wall framed by thick, mahogany columns and filled with black-and-white pictures of street scenes and tin apothecary signs from the '30s and '40s. Below these were three long shelves, brimming with old, glass medicine bottles and boxes, mostly of the snake oil variety.

"Since 1936," Harry said proudly. "And I'm about to make your day, Mr. Ramp. What's the biggest, boldest ad in your book you can buy?"

"The back cover," Damon said, stiffening to a very still position and trying to calm his brain to work this just right. The back cover was still available. "It's the most beautiful ad in the book; glossy, full color—and we have a wonderful graphic arts department. How does showing Rice Apothecary to a half million people grab you?"

"Like this!" Harry said.

Harry started singing "We're in the Money" and did a ballroom dance with an invisible partner behind the counter. He was singing and hooting and hollering with a bubbly happiness that made Damon wonder if the old man was taking more drugs than he was selling—and if so, would he share? But something didn't look right when Harry tried to do a pirouette. He came down really hard, slapping his hand loudly on the counter. Then he gasped, grasping at the air with a trembling arm, an open-mouthed look of fear on his face. It was as though the world stopped, so still was the moment. Then he collapsed.

Damon had the same look on his face. He stood frozen in time, not even breathing. Then he looked around the store for help. He yelled "Help!" but no one answered. He finally snapped out of it and called 911.

The paramedics were there in five minutes and immediately went to work on Harry. They stopped after a few minutes. Their tension released, and they collectively sighed, one of them kicking at the floor. They knew Harry. You could tell. They questioned Damon briefly before hauling Harry away. Damon looked at his cheap plastic watch. The commission on the back cover could have bought him a Rolex.

Seeing someone dead or die has a strange stillness to it. Just about everything becomes meaningless in the face of death. But then you go on, and the meaningless takes on value again. Damon felt that stillness as he stood on the sidewalk outside Rice Apothecary. But his nose had its own agenda. There was a unique smell wafting in on the warm March breeze. His eyes followed suit. Its glazed white brick shone like a pearl in the sun, its blue lettering glimmering like the Tyrrhenian Sea. White Castle was right down the street. *Milah.*

Three

Damon picked up a half dozen hamburgers and some fries and onion chips, and he headed for I-94. He only used the freeway when he was in a hurry, preferring to soften his day with a little sightseeing with all the driving he had to do, the drive up Summit or through Cathedral Hill being so much more pleasant than a freeway wall. He exited on Dale Street and headed down to Grand, then up past Victoria, driving faster than he usually did, his cargo snug in his lap to keep warm. He had the heat blasting to dry out his soggy foot, his shoe off to help speed up the process, an old jacket lining the footwell to keep it from getting any soggier. He would have been in a hurry with or without the cargo or the soggy foot. He hadn't stopped thinking about Milah since he met her.

Damon found a place to park across and down the street from Milah's. He was parked at a slight angle, and could see just part of the small white building under the giant oak. His foot got a shock of cold and damp when he slid his soggy shoe back on, and a couple of test steps revealed a pronounced *squish* he would have to live with the rest of the day. As he was gathering his things to head across the street, he saw a man exiting Milah's. He was fiftyish, tall and well-groomed, wearing a beautiful charcoal gray topcoat with a black silk scarf underneath. Damon had admired a coat just like it at Macy's, and it was worth more than his car. The man kept his head down and moved quickly, but not too fast to be suspicious, and he was empty-handed. Maybe they didn't have what he was looking for. Damon watched him head down the sidewalk, curious to know which car he was going to get into. Trying to match people and their cars was a game Damon played to help pass all the time he spent in his car. He had it narrowed down to three: a blue Mercedes S550, a black Lexus LS 460, and an Infinity Q50, which sported a color from the gunmetal family, which went very well with the man's coat. Damon was guessing the Infinity and smiled when the man slowed by the car. The man admired it briefly, but then quickly crossed the street to a used car lot, filled with a motley mix of ten-year-old cars and a few junkers. He ducked inside a silver Ford Crown Victoria, parked in the jumble of all the other cars. Damon wouldn't have noticed it if the man hadn't gotten in it. It had three little antennas on the trunk.

It didn't look like they were there to catch speeders.

Four

Milah was behind the counter arranging things in the display case when Damon walked in. She looked just like she did yesterday, except she had stepped out of the Doc Martens and into a pair of brown suede boots with short, spiked heels. The high boots disappeared under her long, brown corduroy skirt. And she added a silk scarf, a splash of gold and crimson that took the edge off her goth look. She turned around to see who just walked in her store.

"Can I help you?" she asked, as though she had never seen Damon before.

This didn't surprise Damon, but it still felt insulting. Some people are memorable and some are not. Damon was of the latter variety, and everything about him was average: average height, average clothes, topped with medium brown hair and eyes, which were framed by thick, black glasses that were hardly cutting edge. But one thing made him memorable today.

He held up the bag of White Castles.

"Remember me?" Damon said, confident that that would do the trick. He liked the way that felt. He seldom felt anything remotely close to confidence.

It took a few seconds, but Milah finally smiled. "Well, well, if it isn't the miniature Clark Kent bearing gifts," she said.

Damon had never been called that before, but it wasn't totally insulting. It was kind of funny, really, because there was a slight resemblance to Clark Kent, only Damon was a smaller version, with brown hair and eyes. But the clumsy meekness and hapless nature were there. And Clark Kent was the kind of guy who would step into an ankle-deep pile of slush and have a guy die on him just when he was about to hit pay dirt. But at least he got to make up for it by being Superman.

"Guess you really want that tour," Milah said.

"I'll settle for a little information about your business," Damon said.

"I wear many hats around here. Which one would you like me to put on?"

"Well, we could start with the name of your business," Damon said. "It seems to me that flowers aren't the main part of your business, yet your name clearly connotes flowers. I'm just curious as to why you chose it."

"Well, Clarky, it is rather catchy, is it not? And I like flowers." She motioned to the glass-doored display case, filled with flowers, in the corner. "Do you like flowers?"

"Yes, very much," Damon said. He liked her pet names for him. They made him feel warm and liked. It beat stepping into puddles of slush. "Which varieties do you have in your display case? They look awfully dark."

"Dark isn't necessarily awful, Mr. Kent. And which varieties do you prefer?"

"Orchids, mostly. I'm a regular visitor to the McNeely Conservatory at Como Park. I like the crystal dome, with all the palms and orchids. It's so light and warm and colorful. It's one of my favorite places, especially in winter."

"You're not afraid of the dark, are you?" Milah asked, taking a bite out of her hamburger that cut it in half.

"What makes you say that?"

Damon's bites were half the size of Milah's. And he hated when the whole pickle slice came out when you took a bite. He pulled the pickle slice from his mouth and put it into one of the burger boxes.

"And apparently afraid of pickles, too," Milah said.

She was straight to the point with everything she said or did. Damon admired her strength and wit and the confident way she carried herself. There was a street-smart toughness about her, a strong purpose in everything she did. Qualities that Damon could only aspire to.

"Well?" Milah asked, feigning impatience with a shrug of her shoulders. "Come on, Clarky, try and keep up."

Damon decided against his usual evasiveness and addressed her question head-on. "I guess I never really thought of it in such black-and-white terms. But if you're asking me if I prefer lightness over darkness, I would have to say, 'Yes.'"

"Why? There's so much more complexity and intrigue in the darkness. It's such a closer representation of what life is all about, the mysteries, the big picture, the 'Why are we here?' and 'What's on the other side?' The true power of the universe is in its darkness; in its dark matter and dark energy. And liking orchids and other tropicals is akin to liking puppies. Who doesn't? Way too easy of a button to push."

"But aren't ghosts and apparitions light?" Damon asked. "Darkness and light need each other. It's weight and counterweight—one wouldn't be without the other. And light can be just as intriguing as darkness. In fact, one of my favorite orchids at the conservatory is the *gongora chocoensis*. The flowers look like these little apparitions, all white and ghostly. They almost seem to float, like these otherworldly faerie creatures."

"I'm impressed, Mr. Kent. Scientifically correct and a nicely made point to boot. And I suppose you could also tell me the *gongora's* tribus and subtribus classifications as well?"

"*Cymbidieae* and *stanhopeinae*, I believe. Respectively, of course."

"Well, of course. Well, well, a cigar for the miniature Clark Kent. You do know your flowers. That was hardly a pedestrian observation. Now all we have to do is conquer your fear of the dark and pickles."

"I'll settle for a sale. After all, that is why I'm here."

"Is it now. Do you always go to such great lengths just to make a sale? Hardly an efficient use of an account executive's time. And judging by your appearance and manner, you're not exactly knocking 'em dead, are you?"

"Well, I knocked one dead this morning."

"I guess I stand corrected, then," Milah said. "Big sale?"

"No. A guy died on me—literally. But it could have been one of my biggest. He was all set to buy the back cover."

"You're kidding, right? The guy you were pitching actually died on you?"

"Honest."

"Oh, Clarky, Clarky, what are we gonna do with you?"

"A commission would be nice."

"Would you settle for a tour?"

"Is there a pot of gold at the end of it?"

"No. But it looks like you've got nothing to lose."

Five

Behind the red curtain was a red world trapped in a gauzy neon haze, an atmosphere saturated in red spectrum, its air thick and smoky sweet, somewhere between Mars and Tralfamadore. It was an adults-only Old Navy store on ecstasy, its mannequins dressed in rubber and buckled leather restraints instead of preppy argyle. Its soundtrack was sultry and minor keyed, breathy saxophones underscored by subwoofered bass tones that slithered up your leg and tingled your nether regions. It was a world where people could easily lose their way, and did so on a regular basis.

Damon knew places like this existed, but never allowed himself the visit. He had no moral objections or religious scruples to speak of, it simply was a matter of it not being him; there was no desire to go there. He much preferred the conservatory or a visit to a museum. Damon lived in an insular intellectual world, where things of a sexual nature were out of place. But Milah intrigued him. Human beings intrigued him, although he eschewed any kind of lengthy interpersonal contact. It was like his game of guessing which cars people were going to get into. He was just curious about human nature and what people were up to. And there definitely was something going on with Milah. It was an arousal of curiosity, not sexuality.

"Earth to Clarky. You still with me?" Milah said, prompting Damon to begin reentry protocols.

"Oh my," Damon said.

Milah laughed. "Welcome back. And here we have everything you need for the well-appointed dungeon…"

"Oh my."

"So what classification should we put this under?" Milah asked, spinning around a hooded, leathered mannequin.

"I think we can safely rule out flowers and department stores."

A labyrinth of darkened hallways lined with rooms snaked along the periphery, a slant of light emanating from under one of the doors.

"What's down the hallway?" Damon asked.

"Storage," Milah said.

The echoed sound of a man grunting reverberated from the hallway. A younger voice followed. Damon immediately connected the voice to the teenage boy he had seen at Milah's during his first visit. *It's that boy.*

"Burl must be working back there," Milah said, offering an explanation that Damon didn't ask for. "Had enough, Clarky?"

Milah assumed the answer was yes and headed for the curtain. Damon didn't move. He knew he'd hear the sounds again. Targeting the voices would make them clearer and allow Damon's voice-face file to make a positive ID. The VF file was one of many internal databases housed in Damon's orderly brain. It was a very specific form of OCD that the DSM-5 had yet to classify. He heard the sounds. His hard drive booted.

Match.

"Come on, Clarky, I don't have all day. I've got work to do."

There was a terse edge to her voice. The sarcastic, lighthearted tone was gone. Damon got Milah's message to leave but still didn't move. He heard it again. His VF file went to work on the older man's voice. *Searching criteria…fiftyish, graying, tall, well-groomed…*

"Like that man," Damon said aloud, a neural misfire that caught him by surprise, like a sudden hiccup.

"What?"

Milah went back to Damon and physically guided him in the direction she wanted him to go. Suddenly their leisurely lunch and conversation was hurried. Milah was walking at twice her usual pace and the witty repartee had all but disappeared. She guided Damon to where he'd left his things.

"Thanks for lunch, Clarky. Now go out and make some sales."

"Did I mention the back cover is still available?"

"You just did, and no thanks."

"That didn't sound like Burl back there."

"What's he supposed to sound like? C'mon, off you go..."

Six

Damon sat in his car and began processing what he had just seen and heard. His brain filed the sounds right next to the cover of Burl's magazine. A picture of the boy Damon's VF file ID'd was right next to it, as was the well-dressed man. It was an unforced association; his mind naturally connected things and had a very orderly filing system. Things were always grouped together properly.

Damon checked his day planner for his afternoon appointments. There was only one firm appointment, with a new Vietnamese restaurant—at least it was vaguely firm due to some language barriers with the new owner—and there were two warm calls on the schedule, one step above a cold call, where Damon had made phone contact with the potential clients and was given permission to stop by. Both were in the Midway area and that's where Damon headed. As he drove by the used car lot he checked for the silver Crown Victoria that the well-dressed man had gotten into. It was gone, but it didn't take long for Damon to find it again. It was right behind him.

With its grille lights flashing.

Damon pulled over and eyed the Crown Victoria in his rearview mirror, expecting to see the well-dressed man in the passenger seat, but he was gone. The driver was alone and got out of his car. He was heavyset, with a craggy face and rosy, bulbous nose, topped with silvery, Brylcreemed hair slicked straight back, dressed in a rumpled trench coat over a navy suit. Damon's VF file went to work on the rumpled man. He looked so much like a cop that he might as well have been wearing a patrolman's uniform. Damon pushed the electric window switch to lower the driver's side window. It went about halfway before it locked up crooked, slipping off the track. Damon said hello to Pontiac again and waited to see if he was right about the man's voice.

"Mornin'," the rumpled man said. "Shoppin' today?"

Match.

"Excuse me?"

"Like flowers, do ya?"

The rumpled man sounded just like he looked. And there was a nuance as subtle as a hammer in the way he said "do ya" and dropped his g's. *Definitely Chicago.*

"Yes, as a matter of fact. Very much."

"Not much of a selection, though," the rumpled man said, nodding toward Milah's. "Much better at McNeely, don'tcha think?"

Damon didn't even consider the possibility of a coincidence. He was being followed. Even stranger, he was being *told* he was being followed.

The rumpled man nodded toward Milah's again. "Anything else in there ya like? Odd little store..."

"It was a business call," Damon said. "I sell yellow pages advertising for *NewStar.*"

"See or hear anything unusual in there? Anything jump out at ya or strike you as being odd or out of place? Relatively speaking, of course."

Damon couldn't think of one *usual* thing from his two visits to Milah's.

"No, not really," Damon said.

"Ya goin' back there?"

"I'm not sure."

"Try."

"And if I do?"

"Just let me know if you see anything unusual," the rumpled man said, fishing for something out of his inside pocket. He handed Damon a business card. "Number's on the back."

LUCOVICH IMPLEMENT • AUTHORIZED BOBCAT DEALER

FARM AND CONSTRUCTION EQUIPMENT

SALES • PARTS • SERVICE

MASON, WISCONSIN

Seven

The rumpled man was as likely a purveyor of farm implements as Damon was an NFL nose tackle. As vague as the rumpled man ostensibly seemed, he dropped enough information to light up Damon's brain like Times Square on New Year's Eve. New criteria were added and linked and organized by a simple closing of the eyes and a long relaxing breath. Endorphins released and bathed him in a tingly warmth, and he let it all pour in. Damon left the mesosphere to meet Major Tom.

> *Though I'm past one hundred thousand miles*
> *I'm feeling very still*
> *And I think my spaceship knows which way to go*

Reentry came cold and hard and in the shape of a GMC Yukon, whose curiosity as to what a Pontiac tastes like could no longer be ignored, taking a large bite out of Damon's bumper and left rear fender. A harried soccer mom exited the tank talking and proved incapable of shutting up. Damon got out of his car to inspect the damage and heard all about the woman's bad day. She called the police, and they waited. She said something about hockey practice or the fall of Saigon or getting back on the gold standard, but Damon was too preoccupied with the view that the silver Crown Victoria had previously enjoyed. Across the street and between the buildings was a perfect view of Milah's front door.

The first man who entered was of the Peeping Tom variety, and looked like he might be on the list of registered sex offenders. Burl showed him the door in the time it took the young Gladys Kravitz to kvetch about her neighbor's terrier, which had taken a liking to her lawn. One minute. A carbon copy of the Abercrombie model passed him as he was leaving, and judging by the leer Peeps gave the handsome young boy, he was probably on the dean's list of Level Three perps. Abercrombie got to stay. Five minutes later, a clone of the well-dressed man entered. He stayed too. Maybe there was a dress code. Maybe Milah was up to something even bigger than Damon imagined. The *maybe* was probably no longer necessary.

The police showed up just in the nick of time to save Damon from a ballet recital story or how the Medicis secretly bankrolled the development of the Zamboni. The officer showed about as much interest in the woman's incessant chattering as he did about Milah's.

None.

Eight

The clock struck midnight in Damon's brain, and Guy Lombardo began to ring in 1947.

The rumpled man is definitely law enforcement and probably knows every Tom, Dick, and Peeps who walked through Milah's front door. Probably had pictures. He and the well-dressed man were sweet on Milah's, but there isn't a tool in the toolbox to link them to local Johnny Laws. The Chicago thing's hanging over me like a rain cloud, and that phony business card and third-degree soft-shoe stuck in my craw like a string of chicken between my bicuspids. Then there were the Doublemint twins. The swell-dressers keep coming up target-market types, the kind that have stacks to burn and get invited to all the best parties. And the Abercrombie models look like the kind of party favors that turn up just before a priest's or congressman's career comes to a screeching halt. The area code on the number Rumples gave me is 612, which is Minneapolis, and the farm equipment card is cute as a circus flea's ear. Prefix 201 means that it's a cell, and Johnny Laws make for the dreamiest stalkers. The way Burl showed Peeps the door and guarded the DARK ROOM means that he's local muscle, as if he could be anything else, except maybe something that crawled out from under a rock. Milah is management level, but her slipup of giving me the tour while business was being transacted and the ham-handed way she tried to get me to breeze means that she isn't the brains behind the operation. The Brain wouldn't be a palmist or a florist clerk, or make those kind of mistakes. The sounds coming from the back room were straight out of Mutual of Omaha's Wild Kingdom, *but Marlin Perkins was nowhere to be found, and his partner, Jim, is probably still trying to get that damn python off his leg. It was, at the very least, prostitution. If it involves minors, it kicks it up to federal, which is jake with my hunch that Rumples and the WDM weren't SPPD. And if you're going to play with fire like minors in prostitution you might as well shoot the works.*

Blackmail.

Nine

Damon was still woozy from New Year's when he turned onto University Avenue to call on the Pho House, the Vietnamese restaurant that was sure to guarantee him a lucrative and early retirement, which could begin in earnest if only he could find a place to park. There was one spot available, conveniently located right in front of Mount Everest. Damon wished Pontiac a Happy New Year as he worked his way across the seat, then shuffled backwards against the side of the car trying to make it to the street. Road salt doesn't play well with navy overcoats.

An Asian man standing at a rickety old lectern smiled and bowed in welcoming Damon to the Pho House. Damon said hello to the man and took off his coat to inspect the damage, then began to brush the salt residue off with his hand. The diminutive man was all-too-willing to oblige, and was soon helping Damon brush off his coat, which soon turned into a vigorous beating of his coat that bordered on an assault. Then he abruptly grabbed the coat and charged toward the kitchen, leaving Damon alone, confused, and coatless.

The man returned with the coat a few minutes later and proudly handed it to Damon, proclaiming it to be "good as new." The coat looked like it just came from the dry cleaners, sans the plastic and that dry cleaner's smell, the latter being supplanted by the smell of steamed dumplings, an appetizer whose delicious taste belies its unfortunate odor, which is reminiscent of dirty dishwater.

The man introduced himself as Thao, and Thao was impressed with the brochures and sample ads that Damon showed him, so much so that he seemed to want to buy everything Damon offered him. Damon's inauspicious beginning at the Pho House was getting brighter by the minute, and he would gladly foot the bill for a real dry cleaners if he could make a good sale to Thao.

"Do you deliver?" Damon asked.

"Yes. Liver. Best in town," Thao replied.

Damon grabbed an imaginary steering wheel. "No, deliver—drive?"

"Yes, yes, drive. Toyota. Bad, bad problem. Nasty business."

Damon grabbed a menu and pointed at it. "No, does your restaurant deliver food—drive food to people?"

"Oh, no, no—no drive-through. Eat here."

Damon pulled out his sample phone book and went to the restaurant section. He pointed to a full-page ad with a menu. "For Pho House. Yes?"

"Oh, yes, yes!"

"You buy?"

Thao enthusiastically pointed at the page. "Yes, want. Yes, yes."

Damon wanted to make sure before he started processing the paperwork. "Buy? With money? Yes?"

"Yes, yes—"

"Excuse me, can I be of some assistance?" A Hmong police officer interrupted his lunch to see if he could bridge the communication gap. "What are you selling?"

"Yellow pages advertising, but I'm not sure if he understands it costs money. Can you help?"

The officer started speaking Hmong to Thao. They were both pointing toward the restaurant ad. Thao still sounded enthusiastic, but that quickly turned to the sound of concern. He gave Damon a glaring, suspicious look. A dirty look supersedes all known languages. The interpreter was no longer necessary.

"No, no, you leave now, *salesman*," Thao growled, pointing at the door.

The salt stains returned and Damon's little pine tree was no match for the smell of steamed dumplings.

Damon's next call at a trophy shop took all of two minutes, about as much time as you would need to confirm a name, address, and phone number, and a quick scrawl on a preprinted contract to verify that he made the call. Atlas Upholstery took twenty minutes, eighteen of which were spent waiting. Al's Taxidermy could wait. No use in running across town to get another door slammed in your face. It's better to have three or four doors in the same neighborhood slammed in your face, a much more efficient use of an account executive's time. *Milah.*

It was another fast food lunch in the car courtesy of the dollar menu, of which Damon was a frequent patron, due mostly to necessity. A battle of odorous titans was taking place inside his car, the smell of the Fast Food Kings taking on the powerful Pho House Giants. It was like the Flyers taking on the Bruins.

Scenery is important to digestion, and Damon was only eight minutes from Mounds Park, a favorite of his that offered a beautiful view of the Saintly City and the Mississippi. The planes taking off and landing from Holman Field were a cool bonus. But Damon had a different view in mind today, one that he just had previously enjoyed. It was a popular spot for rumpled and well-dressed men alike. The people-watching there was fast becoming the best in town. But Damon was getting an internal alert from his in-house database. It had a curious Chicago dialect. *Much better at McNeely, don'tcha think?*

Ten

If a mouse is about to follow a cat, then he better wear a pretty good disguise. And if it's a big, old Chicago alley cat like Rumples, he better be up to the task and understand the risks.

The best disguise Damon could come up with meant a visit to his mother's. His smashed up Bonneville would be as easy to spot as traces of cocaine and hookers in Charlie Sheen's system, and the smell of stale cigarettes and must in mom's gold 1979 Lincoln Town Car was a quantum improvement over the Kings vs. Giants match still playing out in Damon's car.

His mother's car had its own unique set of quirks. You had to work the left turn signal manually, and the driver's seat was stuck in a semi-reclined position. When his mother drove the car, all you could see was the top of her blue-gray head over the steering wheel. And two parking spots and a yacht master were necessary to dock the 19-footer. But at least both of her doors worked. Her ashtray was so full of half-smoked, lipstick-stained butts that it was incapable of being closed. The backseat was a warehouse full of things from her garage sale adventures. Bags of clothes, books, lamps, pictures, tennis rackets, a couple of persimmon woods, and a Coleman lantern was just the stuff Damon could see. It was a rolling garage sale in itself. But the Bushnell binoculars might come in handy.

Damon settled into the spot he had previously parked before his first visit to Milah's. Rumples wasn't at his post in the used car lot. The reclined seat was in a perfect position for staking out a place. Damon grabbed the binoculars and slid into position.

The customer flow for the first half hour was a mixed bag of goth kids, guilty-looking suburban dads—chiropractic visits forthcoming from looking back and forth so many times—and the occasional trench-coated peep. The classics never go out of style. But the well-dressed man that entered aroused Damon's full attention. Others, too.

The well-dressed man put into motion a curious choreography of foot traffic around Milah's. Suddenly the population on the sidewalks that surrounded her shop increased by at least a half dozen. Damon's hard drive booted up and began separating the passersby from the ones who paid particular attention to the store. He flagged four on foot. And when Damon checked to see if Rumples was checking in too, he noticed a man in a third-floor window of the apartments behind the used car lot. He had a camera. He made five. But most curious of all was the ten-year-old boy lurking in the trees with a cell phone camera. One in the grassy knoll, one in the School Book Depository, and four on the street. And when Rumples reported for duty it all rolled into a nice, fat seven. A natural. But the kid had moved to the front of the line. The cat would have to wait.

The notion of a ten-year-old blackmailer just didn't jive. But the fact that he had a camera meant that he was an information gatherer. He was easy to follow, as ten-year-olds have yet to develop stealth capabilities. He walked just like a little kid would walk down the sidewalk. Slow, shuffling gait, occasionally stopping to soccer around a snow chunk. He even threw his hands up in celebration when he scored an imaginary goal.

He stopped at a buddy's on Chatsworth and knocked on the door. The buddy that opened the door was anything but. He looked about fifteen, had long, dark hair, wore an old army jacket, and had a pair of headphones wrapped around his neck. It wasn't a social visit. It was an exchange. The ten-year-old handed him the camera and got a little candy money for the effort. Damon noted the address and went back to his post. It was the first time in six months that Damon had something to do on a Friday night.

Eleven

There was a lion's den somewhere, and Damon vowed to find it. He settled in for the night. So did Rumples. Damon was hungry and wished he had brought some coffee. He started poking around the interior of his mom's yacht for something to help pass the time and maybe provide a little nutrition. A granola or candy bar, some breath mints, anything. The quarry was in the glove box. A pint of Old Crow and some fun-sized Snickers, which were as hard as rocks from the Mesozoic era. The Old Crow was nicely aged. It had a banded tax seal over the top, and they hadn't done that since the 1970s. It was nice to know that Mom was a moderate drinker. And it was frightening to know that Mom was navigating the USS *Lincoln* with questionable eyesight and a snootful of bourbon.

It was a bustling Friday night in the uptown area, with heavy traffic up and down Grand, and people with lives and restaurant reservations, laughing over drinks and sharing war stories after throwing off the yoke of another workweek. Damon had a drink too, about a tablespoon's worth of Old Crow, before putting it back in the glove box. His lips and tongue still burned ten minutes later. But the internal warmth felt good, so he knocked back another, then went to work on one of the Snickers bars. The disparate tastes played surprisingly well together. Chalk up another one for Mom. Damon battened down the hatches and dropped anchor. The sandman made his appointed rounds.

Damon awoke just in time to watch the dance of the shadow people. The strange choreography that was put in motion before by the WDM entering Milah's was back, except this time it played out in the dark. Damon didn't know what put things in motion this time, but it looked almost identical to the first go-round. The people looked and moved the same, like they were shadowy doppelgängers of the first crew. But there was a last-minute replacement off the bench, and he just strode past Damon's starboard side. It was the kid with the army jacket and long hair, out for a stroll with his laptop. He stopped at a bus stop bench and sat down, but he didn't open his laptop, and his chances of finding a bus this time of night was about as good as Damon being named salesman of the year. He was waiting for something. Or someone.

It was a someone, and he was impeccably dressed, moving quickly toward a white Buick LaCrosse, which he ducked into, started, and drove away all inside of ten seconds, making a U-turn to get to Grand and waiting to hang a left. The kid started walking up Grand. As soon as the kid moved, Damon moved, too, like your leg jumps up when Dr. Kildare checks your reflexes. No thought. Just reaction. Rumples would have to wait. Again.

The Buick made the first right and then another, pulling into a parking lot of a small complex of condominiums, with an ivy-lined courtyard that was filled with nice cars. Damon drove by and turned around at the next intersection and parked and waited. The kid came strolling up the street a few minutes later, like he had all the time in the world. The kid turned into the same parking lot and disappeared into the darkness of the side of the building. Dr. Kildare checked Damon's other leg, and soon both legs were up and walking on the sidewalk toward the building.

The kid was leaning against the side of the building, his face conveniently spotlighted by the glow of his laptop. There were flashes of light and movement in the third-floor windows above him. Restless movement, as though the guy were nervous. It was an odd place for a kid to check his Facebook page. Damon kept on walking until he hit Grand, then he doubled back. The kid was still there. Damon's hard drive booted up and went to his probability-correlations file. The PC file was a simple deductive program; you input all available data, then it deduces the most likely scenario. It was a very orderly process of elimination and Damon had the answer before he went back aboard ship.

The kid was hacking.

Twelve

Damon probed a little deeper. The guy the kid was hacking wasn't just your average Joe naïvely broadcasting his wireless signal to everyone within a hundred feet of his home office. The guy was one of the WDMs, and it wasn't much of a stretch to conclude that his business in and around Milah's was likely something that he would prefer to keep to himself. And something was making him extremely nervous. The probabilities and correlations were adding up nicely, and they all seemed to center around the kid with the laptop just kicking back on the side of the building.

Damon's internal databases were being flooded with so much new information and scenarios that he had to close his eyes to let everything get updated. It was Times Square on New Year's all over again, and Damon rang in the new year with a toast. Snickers and Old Crow. Happy New Year, Mom.

Clack clack clack.

He looked like he was about twelve, with a cute turned-up nose and freckles. Not the kind of date that Damon had hoped for on New Year's, but the conversation might be interesting. Damon buzzed down the electric window on the starboard side.

"Dude, it's like being followed by the *Beverly Hillbillies* jalopy. What the fuck. You got Granny stashed in there somewhere, homes? Elly May be better."

It was the kid with the long hair in the army jacket.

"You gonna let me in or am I gonna hafta jack this jalopy?"

Damon unlocked the door and the kid hopped in.

"Fucking freezing, man. Hey—bum me the hooch, homes."

"I'm going to have to see some ID," Damon asked.

"'Bout time you chimed in, Jethro. C'mon, man, medicinal, bro."

Damon handed the kid the bottle. The kid took a drink like a wino from the Bowery. He pulled out his phone and called up some pictures.

"So here's you in front of my house...here's you on stakeout at Petal...and here's a nice shot of your plates—that I'm gonna turn on your ass if you don't tell me why the fuck you're following me around."

"Because smart-aleck, potty-mouthed little extortionists intrigue me," Damon said.

"Good answer, homes. Am I to be threatened by your latter statement," the kid said, mimicking Damon's voice.

"No. The aforementioned was meant to pique your curiosity," Damon said, seeing the kid's mimic and raising it a snobby chip. "Is my point well taken?"

"Indubitably," the kid said. "So where we at, Jethro?"

"Might I suggest a symbiotic arrangement?"

"What's in it for me, homes? I'm guessing most of the symbiosing is gonna be coming from me."

"What's in it for you is that I'm not gonna rat your ass out. *Comprende*, Jed?"

"You're all right, homes."

"Indubitably." Damon extended his hand. "Damon Ramp."

"Hadji."

Thirteen

It took all of five minutes for Damon to conclude that Hadji was as cunning as a James Bond villain and held his liquor like a CIA operative in Cold War Moscow. He was technologically savvy and was putting his skills to work in a fashion that was anything but above board. But it was the relaxed manner that most impressed Damon. It was all just a stroll through the park for Hadji.

"I'm guessing you weren't doing your homework on the side of that building," Damon said.

"Sure I was," Hadji said. He looked at Damon. His eyes were full of mischievous glint.

"You like to collect pictures, too. And it's admirable that you employ locally. Paying minimum wage, I hope."

"Gotta take care of your peeps, Jethro."

"There are others, too—collecting pictures, I mean."

"Grand Central, bro. Like bees around a hive."

"All like-minded, like you?"

"Ain't nobody like me. They're fucking rubes, and they're gonna go down like dominoes. Only so many slices in a pie, man."

"How?"

Hadji tapped his laptop. "Because rubes think firewalls are impenetrable and wouldn't know a packet sniffer from a fucking shih tzu. And they're stupid enough to put all their personal information on their desktop. Everyone's wireless and they just plug 'em in and go without setting up the moats and gates. They're broadcasting like fucking radio stations."

"How many players on the field?"

"You kiddin' me? Enough for a game at Yankee Stadium."

"Did you spot the umpire?"

"You mean Eliot Ness in the Crown Vic? His disguise is about as good as yours."

"FBI?"

"Ya think? Try and keep up, homes."

"What do you know about Milah's operation?"

"Who? Oh, the goth babe. She's hot—but every time I go in for a closer look, baldy throws me out of the store. The operation? Pretty boys and rich guys. Do the math."

"Perhaps a little blackmail, too?"

"Wow. Can't throw one by you."

"But it's not Milah's operation. Any guesses, smart guy?"

"Yeah. The kind of guys that leave the gun and take the cannoli."

"Guess that makes it federal enough." Damon drifted off, sifting through the particulars.

"What's on your mind, homes? I can hear that hamster wheel cranking from here."

"If you're the law, say, going after a drug operation, who would you rather pinch, the street dealer, his supplier, or the cartel behind the supplier?"

"The law is going to try and snag 'em all. But the poor street fuck and his customers are probably the only ones who'll do any time—pretty fucked up if you ask me. But the big fish is always the prize."

"Isn't it curious that no one's been arrested yet? I mean, everyone knows what's going on, right? Why aren't they moving on minors in prostitution? That's huge, and they're letting it go. Not seeing any local cop interest either, like it's a keep-away zone. Why?"

"You're on a roll, Jethro, you tell me."

"Logic dictates that there's more than our eyes can see. Somebody's fishing."

"Waiting for the big fish? Could be. All that other shit could just be chum in the water, waiting for the great white. And whitey's gonna come sniffin' around eventually to see what's what, and they ain't big on sharing."

"Eyes on the prize."

Fourteen

Hadji wasn't interested in the primary players involved in Milah's operation. He was a cottage industry, sniping the minor players one at a time. The WDMs got precedence because they all had something to hide and enough money to keep it hidden. To Hadji, their promiscuous activities were nothing but an attention getter, a useful tool in keeping them paranoid and away from the cops. His main target was their finances, where he could wreak all kinds of damage. He already had bagged one WDM, who conveniently kept all his portfolio information in his Quicken file. Bank accounts. Mutual funds. Pin codes. Even pie charts to track the best performers. Hadji got a down payment and kept all the guy's info, which he could access at will. And the guy had a wife and kids. It was like Christmastime. Hadji said he could practically retire on this guy alone. But Hadji liked the game better than he liked the money, which meant that he wasn't greedy. Which meant that he could keep playing the game, so the money would come anyway. The rubes who were thinking about trying their hand at blackmail would be toyed with like a well-fed cat toys with a mouse. He didn't need the meal. It was just instinct and a question of principle. Hadji was just keeping his claws sharp.

While Hadji was busy playing the game, Damon was preoccupied with why the game was being played like it was. There were just too many players. There was either an unprecedented spike in entrepreneurial extortion or the players were connected.

But the results from Damon's PC file were inconclusive. Common sense told Damon that that many people operating independently was unlikely, but then there was the exception of Hadji and his pint-sized crew. And if there's one operating independently, there's a strong probability of another doing the same. *Results inconclusive...*

Damon was tired and frustrated and shut everything down for the night. The cheese sandwich and glass of milk helped quiet his stomach, and he retired to his recliner and curled up with his favorite afghan in hopes that his mind would follow suit. He closed his eyes and focused on cool, soothing thoughts, which usually involved some type of water. A mountain lake, a quiet brook, an ocean sunset *could just be chum in the water.*

So much for that idea.

Chum just doesn't jump out of the bucket and into the water. Someone was chumming and it sure wasn't Chief Brody. Or Hooper or Quint. Damon agreed with Hadji about the powers behind Milah's operation. The big fish. Damon didn't need to fire up his PC file for this one. Everything just dropped into place as orderly as the biblical account of creation. He thought about giving Hadji a call to share his epiphany, but decided to keep this one for himself, at least for a while. Damon smiled and finally relaxed, widening his grin at the notion of maybe even getting some sleep. He didn't look much like a fisherman, but there was an obvious benefit to employing the skills of a chameleon. There was more going on at Milah's than just your garden-variety stakeout. Damon put a fishing hat on him, like you would put a cherry on a sundae.

Rumples.

Fifteen

If you want to get the mob's attention, there's no better way than to try and cut in on their action. This is their domain, and they don't share with nobody. They don't even like to share with their own people, and they're very efficient at making people go away. Why settle for a piece of the pie when you can have the whole pie for yourself? And the last place you want to be is on the business end of the kind of attention they'll give you. Nobody skims the skim. Nobody.

If Damon was right, then Rumples was playing a very dangerous game. This was a high-stakes game of cat and mouse, except in this case the mouse was nearly as big as the cat, and they all liked to play with guns. Hadji's analogy of chumming was apt as well. Except Rumples was chumming the waters with planted blackmailers instead of chopped up fish and blood. Human bait. A very dangerous game. Mixed metaphors aside, whether it's a great white or a fat, greedy cat, the bait is irresistible. Attention would follow with mathematical certitude. Nobody skims the skim.

But the relaxation Damon had was short-lived. The sense of accomplishment and enjoyment from the release of euphoric neurotransmitters bathing his highly attuned brain was suddenly overcome by a swallowing paranoia. He was so busy figuring out the game that he overlooked a simple glaring fact, which bolted him out of his chair.

He was part of the game, too. And Hadji was in even deeper.

The paranoia had manifested itself into frantic pacing around his apartment. He turned the lights out and began peeking out his windows. He felt he was being watched, like how you know when someone is staring at you. You can just *feel* it. He replayed in his mind his involvement in the game, which only made matters worse. His multiple appearances in and around Milah's had made him a player on the field. He knew Rumples knew about him. But now he wondered who else knew about him. It was an unpleasant wondering, because it involved the last kind of attention you would ever want. Damon changed his mind about calling Hadji.

"Ya know, Jethro, if you wanna play cloak-and-dagger, we really gotta work on the cloaking thing. Dude, it's called caller ID. Plus, you're driving all over town in that fucking jalopy. WTF, man."

"You might want to work on your cloaking abilities too, Hadji. Better still, just stop everything you're doing and just disappear."

"What's on your mind, homes?"

"You were right about what you said. Remember what you said about someone chumming for the great white? Well, I think I know who's doing the fishing."

"So, ya gonna share or we gonna do-si-do some more?"

"What if I told you Eliot Ness was our fisherman?"

"What if I told you that you could just ask him yourself?"

"What?"

"Hello, Mr. Ramp, nice to talk to you again. Special Agent Charles. Someone will be knocking on your door in thirty seconds. He will ask you to come with him. I strongly suggest that you do."

Knock knock knock.

"He's early," Damon said.

"Lucky for you," Charles said. "You have no idea."

Sixteen

He was six feet three inches tall and two hundred twenty-five pounds if he was an ounce. He had close-cropped dark blond hair with no part and wore a crisp gray suit over a white shirt and solid navy tie. He had an earpiece in his right ear and was as stoic as a Doric column. Mid-thirties. Clean, light complexion. Blue eyes. Nordic descent, except customized at the factory in Quantico, Virginia. Maybe Special Forces background. Rangers or SEALs. Rumples was wrong. He didn't ask Damon to come with him. He didn't speak and probably rarely had to. His suit was unbuttoned for quick access to his shoulder holster. Right side. He was a lefty. He gestured with an open, guiding right hand, his left hand kept free, just in case. Textbook. Professional. It was a gesture that silently said, "This way." There were three more just like him, one on one end of the corridor, the other two covering the opposite end by the steps. Damon had never felt safer or more excited or more scared shitless, all at the same time. It was the first time he had plans on a Friday night in six months. When it rains, it pours.

It was a silent, fast-paced scrum out of Damon's apartment building. Damon was in the middle, with two agents in front and two bringing up the rear. Fore and aft. All compass points covered. The formation broke to file into a black Chevy Suburban, but the compass points remained covered. Four doors. Four agents. But they all arrived at their assigned doors at the same time, the two in the front quickening their pace to get to the driver's side doors. Efficient. Silent. Damon in the middle of the backseat, surrounded by a blanket of federal agents. Bang bang. Gone. The Doric man broke radio silence: "Package capture." Eight minutes on west I-94. Fifth Street exit to Washington Avenue South. West, to an office building parking lot and straight into an underground garage. Whisked out in the same manner and brought to a small room with a table and four chairs. One window, smoked glass. Closed the door. Bang bang. Gone.

Damon straightened his back and brought his heels together, clasping his hands and resting them on the cold metal table. He closed his eyes for a systems update, his orderly mind backing up and organizing his internal files, his brain warm and tingly from neurotransmission. He opened his eyes to greet his visitor, who was fast approaching. Ten seconds, give or take. He was right on time. Damon smiled, still seeing him in an old fishing hat. And he brought coffee, too.

"Good morning, Mr. Ramp," Rumples said, sliding one of the cups in front of Damon.

"Good morning, Special Agent Charles, and thank you."

"Usually, reading at this time of night puts me to sleep," Rumples said. "But I just read the most fascinating story."

"I surmise this story somehow involves me," Damon said.

"Honestly, Mr. Ramp—a salesman? You are somewhat underemployed, are you not?"

"So I've been told."

"So, tell me, how does a guy with damn-near perfect ACT and SAT scores, an IQ off the charts, full-ride scholarships to Princeton and MIT—and recruited by the CIA—get to sell yellow pages advertising? Which, I might add, you're not very good at."

"Because I like flowers."

"Mathematics, too. The CIA recruited you for your work in stochastic analysis. We're not talking freshman algebra here, are we?"

"Probability theory. And my ACT was a perfect 36."

"So dazzle me, Mr. Perfect 36. What does the CIA do with a number cruncher like you?"

"I crunched intelligence data, not just raw numbers. But statistical correlations and probability distributions would logically follow. Basically, the CIA was just trying to figure out how the bad guys worked. As random as everyone thinks they are, correlations were always found. Spikes in certain activities invariably begat spikes in other areas. I helped connect the dots and flag the red herrings."

"But Nine-Eleven happened anyway."

"Yes."

"That's it? Yes?"

"Yes. You know the rest of the story."

"We had him."

"It never should have happened."

"And you washed out of Intelligence shortly thereafter."

"The writing was on the wall. After Nine-Eleven, the cowboys took over. They were seeing red and stopped listening altogether. It became an exercise in futility. Then Iraq dropped out of the clear blue, which had everyone in my world scratching their heads. It was time to leave."

"Let's segue to our current situation. You've aroused some attention by parties of interest involved in a federal investigation. And you know you've obstructed justice in more ways than you really want me to mention. You're a brilliant man, Mr. Ramp, so I'm going to give you the benefit of the doubt as to what your next move should be."

"You mean, keep up the good work?"

"Good night, Mr. Ramp."

Seventeen

There was something about their conversation that turned all Damon's circuits on. There was a purpose and a subtext to everything Rumples said, and Damon began decoding protocols. He began to walk the room to increase his blood flow, the addition of caffeine to the process akin to an F-18 going to afterburners. It was a test *ACT and SAT scores* and a challenge *So dazzle me, Mr. Perfect 36* and the green light was given *I'm going to give you the benefit of the doubt as to what your next move should be.* The VIP treatment by the federal agents was meant to convey a message as well. *We got your back.*

Probability One: Damon was just given license to operate at his own discretion, and the feds would have his back.

You mean, keep up the good work?

Exactly.

But maybe not.

Probability Two had a strange chill attached to it. It had weight and moved slowly. The afterburners kicked off. Truth and reality have a greater gravity, and it brought Damon back to his chair. It was a quiet deduction, moored by a nineteenth-century scientific and philosophic rule proposed by some guy named Occam: *Entities should not be multiplied unnecessarily...explanations of unknown phenomena should be sought first in terms of known quantities.*

It was a ruse.

Rumples wanted the mob to grab Damon. He wanted information. They didn't have his back. The show with the federal agents was just that: A show—a dazzling piece of choreography put on just for Damon's benefit. A false sense of security, the reddest of red herrings. All the compliments, the deference...he was just being stroked. Rumples was chumming the waters with planted blackmailers in hopes of drawing out the great white. And now he wanted Damon to jump in the chum bucket. Human bait. A very dangerous game.

But Damon couldn't get his mind around why he was such a strong party of interest. He knew he was being singled out, but it just didn't make sense. He was clearly not a money player as far as threatening the mob's operation. Not even a whisper of a hint of a threat. Yet, of all the players on the field, they chose him. Rumples's dog-and-pony show worked off that premise, and all but confirmed it. All of Damon's internal databases and programs came up empty. No logical deductions could be made. *Results inconclusive...*

Eighteen

"What did you find out?"

"Petal is bleeding all over the place."

"Are our inside people grifting?"

"I don't think so."

"I didn't ask for your opinion. Are they grifting?"

"No."

"Then who is?"

"There's this kid hacking our clients."

"Is he connected?"

"No."

"He goes away."

"Understood."

"Who are the others?"

"There are several interested parties, but only two have moved. And the feds grabbed the guy."

"The salesman?"

"Yes. His name is Damon Ramp."

"His name is Damonico Aloicious Naimo."

"Family?"

"*Mia famiglia.*"

"Sir?"

"He's my brother."

Nineteen

He was five feet six inches tall and any guess under two hundred pounds wouldn't win you any prizes. His thin, gray hair came up short considering the square footage it had to cover, and he wore a pair of limp gray coveralls over, hopefully, something other than body hair. He had a bulky hearing aid in his left ear and was as soft as an overripened tomato. Mid-fifties. Ruddy, whiskied complexion. Brown eyes. Italian descent, stock factory all the way. He was either maintenance or motor pool. He didn't speak and it probably wouldn't be of any interest anyway. He gestured with a tired wave, a gesture that silently said, "C'mon, I haven't got all night." Damon had never felt more underwhelmed or bored senseless, all at the same time. At least he had a ride home.

It was a silent ride most of the way, sans for the overnight radio talk about Bigfoot, possibly a distant cousin of the hirsute driver. The car was a retired Crown Vic, stripped of all its law enforcement accoutrements, but still a solid driver. Traffic on I-94 was about what you would expect at three AM, and they sailed right through to the Mounds Boulevard exit, up Third Street, right on Maria, up to Hudson Road, and Damon was home.

Damon didn't think much of the fact that the man knew where to go. But that also meant the man had been briefed, and Damon felt that something else was coming. It came in the form of a note the man pulled from his front pocket. It simply said KEEP UP THE GOOD WORK.

Then the man got out of the car and started walking down the street.

Damon sat in the passenger seat and watched the man walk about a hundred feet before hopping into a dark sedan. Bang bang. Gone. Damon was being given the car for a reason, and his PC file spit out the answer almost simultaneously with the thought: The car was bugged. Most assuredly had a tracking device. Then his internal alarm sounded.

There was one more something-else.

He was in so fast that Damon couldn't make out his dimensions. He was dark, wore dark colors, didn't speak, and every move he made was with lightning precision. It was a type of precision similar in efficiency to the feds, but with more of a street edge to it. Less polish, but equally effective. Slight hint of menace. The guy could handle himself. Tough guy.

Wiseguy.

They were on I-35E heading north out of the city inside of five minutes. Damon was more curious than frightened. Staving off the fear was the simple fact that he was of no threat to anyone in any way, shape, or form. He had questions, but knew the answers would be forthcoming. But he thought a casual conversation might be fun. You don't get a chance to talk to a wiseguy every day.

"May I—"

"Shut up."

Not as fun as he thought.

Guido pulled out a blindfold from his inside pocket and handed it to Damon. It was a sleeping mask, the kind they used to wear on old game shows. They should have just called them game show masks, because no one ever used them for sleeping.

"Seriously?" Damon asked.

"Shut up or I go to option two."

It smelled of lavender with a hint of the man's cologne and something else. There was a strange softness to the smell. It was pleasant, but complex and dense.

One minute after the blindfold Guido pulled over. Damon's door swung open and someone grabbed him by the arm and pulled him out of the car. They got into another car and were gone in ten seconds.

Wiseguys.

The leather seat was warm and soft and smelled nice. And mixed with the scent of the mask...

Good night, Mr. Ramp.

Twenty

The leather couch was warm and soft and had that rich chocolatey smell that only the finest Italian leather has. The pillows and blankets were of equal quality, all pastel yellows and greens, with thread-counts at the top of the scale. There was a mahogany serving tray on the coffee table with two covered platters of floral china and a matching coffee pot, fresh-squeezed orange juice in a crystal tumbler. Thick-cut bacon and scrambled eggs and French toast. Next to the serving tray were copies of the *Washington Post, New York Times, Wall Street Journal,* and *USA Today,* fanned out neatly, a copy of the *Pioneer Press*—Damon's favorite paper—resting on top.

Damon propped himself up on the couch and booted up his operating systems for the day. The sun was streaming in through six large picture windows that ran from floor to ceiling, an oval configuration that provided a panorama of forests and water. Big water. The ore carrier in the distance safely ruled out Mille Lacs.

Lake Superior.

Damon's systems were up and running and in need of their morning run. He opened up his geography profiles program. The GP file was his version of Google Earth, and it began streaming data on the big lake: *Area, 31,700 square miles; length, 382 statute miles, east to west; width, 160 statute miles, north to south; maximum depth, 1,333 feet; volume, 3 quadrillion gallons; average water temperature, 40 degrees Fahrenheit (4.4 degrees Celsius); renewal time, 199 years. Borders Michigan, Minnesota, Wisconsin, and Ontario, Canada.*

Damon's PC file immediately ruled out Michigan and Canada. He was either in Minnesota or Wisconsin. If he had been awake during his trip he would have known, blindfold or not. He knew the drive and all the towns along the way by heart. His internal clock and GP file would have broken down minutes to miles. He had played the game once with his stepfather on a drive up north when he was a boy. His eyes closed, he calculated exactly where they were, from St. Paul to Duluth. No matter. Breakfast was getting cold.

Damon studied his surroundings while he ate. It was an oval, teak-paneled room with built-in bookshelves filled with beautiful, hardcover volumes. The library. There was a large, ornately carved black desk resting on a Persian rug, set back in the deepest part of the room. Impressionist oil paintings hung on the far wall. They looked real; significant. His breakfast was still warm.

Breakfast was as delicious as it was well presented, and was finished with the finest cup of coffee Damon had ever tasted. Hazelnut. With real cream in the floral creamer. Damon passed on the newspapers, instead picking up a coffee table book on Impressionist art. He came across J.M.W. Turner's *Seascape: Folkestone*, and then he looked up. He looked down again, then he looked up. One more time. *Private collection, New York.*

It had moved.

It was right next to the Monet.

Damon went over for a closer look, the large art book cradled in his arms. If it was a reproduction, it was a damn good one. The paint was thick with texture and depth. The swirls and dabs of the brush strokes seemed haphazard up close, a seeming hasty blur of brushwork. But from a proper distance they were perfection. It emanated light, almost as though illuminated from within. He repeated the process one more time.

"Yes, it's real."

She had entered the room without a sound. Her hands were clasped behind her back as she approached Damon. Beautifully tailored cream linen slacks with a French yellow blouse. Shoulder-length auburn hair and dark eyes. Probably forties, but she looked younger. Creamy, flawless skin. She smelled wonderful.

"Do you like Turner?" she asked. Her head was tilted curiously. Her shoulder was almost touching Damon's, as she settled alongside. Unusually close for a stranger, she radiated warmth. Damon felt it. It was comfortable and felt very natural.

"It's luminous," Damon said. "So beautiful and complex. The brushwork is dazzling."

"Yes it is. So, I'm assuming you do."

"Do what?"

She giggled. "Like Turner, silly. It's okay. Dumbstruck is a typical reaction."

"I've never seen a masterpiece up close before. It's astonishing. I'm at a loss for words."

"Actually, you gave a very apt observation before," she said.

"Before what?"

She giggled again. "You're wonderfully silly." She put her arm around him and gave him a squeeze. "I'm going to love having you around, Damon."

"No fair," Damon said.

"What's not fair?"

"That you seem to know me and I haven't a clue who you are or where I am—and exactly how long are you going to have me around?"

"It's Maricella."

"Where am I, Maricella?"

"The rest you'll have to get from my brother."

Twenty One

It was long past breakfast, the museum tour had concluded, the newspapers were read, and the nap wasn't working. Damon was surrounded by nothing but beauty, but it was starting to feel like nothing more than a well-appointed prison. Although it wasn't expressed explicitly, Damon surmised that he was to wait for Maricella's brother. Presumably he was the man with the answers, and probably the man who sat behind the hand-carved desk on the Persian rug that was worth more than Damon's family's entire net worth.

But the wait had become interminable. It was time to see if he was prisoner or houseguest.

Time to see what was outside those doors.

Damon still wasn't sure of his status, but at least he was allowed to leave his room. He found himself in the foyer, but you wouldn't get any argument if you called it a rotunda. The crystal chandelier hovered twenty-five feet off the ground and resembled the mothership from *Close Encounters of the Third Kind*. It was at least another ten feet to its base, a ceiling medallion large enough to hold court in the state Capitol. The floor was black and gray granite mixed with variegated tans and creams, large tiles about three feet square. The ceiling medallion was mirrored by a marbled mosaic medallion in the granite, master craftsmanship of the highest order. There were rose windows and stained glass set against the fieldstone, and large portraiture of Italian nobility gracing the periphery, almost as though standing guard.

And an old man in a wheelchair at the end of the room.

The old man sat perfectly still as Damon walked over to meet him. Damon thought he was asleep at first, but his dark eyes were open and focused, and focused on Damon's every step. He looked to be about ninety, and was bundled up in a bulky mix of sweaters and blankets, the only flesh visible being his bony liver-spotted hands and a gaunt face and crown, with thin strands of white hair wisping over more liver spots before falling over his ears. His lips were pursed and blue, but his eyes seemed warm and pleased.

Damon stopped about two feet from the old man, bowed slightly and simply said "Hello."

The old man gestured with his hand for Damon to come closer, mouthing the word "closer" with the movement. Damon moved toward him and crouched by his side. He lifted his hand so Damon could rest his on the arm of the chair and be closer to him. Every movement he made required a Herculean effort.

The old man gestured again as though he wanted to say something. Damon leaned in and placed his ear closer to his mouth.

"Damonico."

Twenty Two

The old man seemed so frail that Damon refrained from asking him all the questions he had, starting with why he had just been called "Damonico." Damon let him take the lead in the communication department, in hopes that he might learn something.

The old man gestured toward Damon's face and tried to whisper something. He was looking intently at Damon, then blinked his eyes twice. Damon's intuition kicked in, and he removed his glasses. The old man blinked his eyes again and nodded slightly, a gesture that said he was pleased. He just wanted to see Damon's eyes. Damon sensed a thousand questions by looking into the old man's eyes, but he just was too weak to ask any of them. All he could do was look at Damon and pat his hand. Damon focused on the old man's eyes, to see what they were saying. They were filled with longing and pain and regret. But the wounds were old, and the old man seemed at peace.

A casually but well-dressed man came out from a foyer door behind the old man and grasped the handles of the wheelchair. He looked serious and concerned, and Damon sensed a degree of irritation, as though the old man were somewhere he wasn't supposed to be. Then it occurred to Damon that the old man might have been coming to see him. Another hour or two, he might have made it to the other side of the foyer.

"Please wait in the library," the serious man said.

He began pushing the old man out of the foyer and into another room. There was a smoothness in his movement, a strength and assuredness. Fortyish, dark hair and eyes, handsome and trim, a shade over six feet. Impeccably groomed and dressed, emanating affluence and privilege and power. There was presence and gravitas.

Damon was back to where he started from. But he had a visitor while he was away. The bedding and the dishes had been removed, and the room had been straightened. But there was only one set of doors in the library, and whoever had straightened the room had not come through the foyer. There was a service entrance somewhere in the room. And it was very well-hidden. Damon was intrigued and smiled, his brain tingly warm with neurotransmission. All circuits on. He imagined all sorts of secret passageways and rooms and hidden doors in the big old house. It was like giving a child a long-awaited puzzle. He began to scan the room in search of possibilities.

Damon's search was cut short by the return of the serious man. He settled in behind the desk as a king would seat himself at his throne.

"I love my father," the serious man said, clasping his hands together. "And I will do anything for him, even though I may disagree. But a dying father's wish is inviolate. And I intend to fulfill that obligation."

"That was a beautiful soliloquy," Damon said. "But it could have been spoken without me even being in the room. If I may, is there an explanation as to why I'm here, floating around somewhere in that nebulous obligation?"

"There may be." The serious man smiled. He seemed pleased with Damon's response. "Conditional, of course."

"Of course."

"My sister enjoyed your visit."

"As did I," Damon said. "She also hinted that you might have some answers for me. Let's start with a couple of easy ones: Who are you people and why am I here?"

"Oh, Mr. Ramp—and I was so enjoying our cordial joust."

"Sorry," Damon said. "And I'm not so sure if jousting with you is a very good idea. You might have a lance under that desk. And there's a strong likelihood that you may have used one before."

"Surely a man of your intellect must have at least formulated an idea as to the answers you seek, am I wrong in assuming that?"

"Okay, let's try that again: Who are you and why am I here?"

Maricella entered the room.

"Antonio, just cut the pissing contest and tell him what he wants to know," she said.

"Yeah," Damon piped in. "What she said."

"And deprive myself the pleasure of engaging an intellect the caliber of Mr. Ramp's? How else am I to gauge his highly regarded abilities? Oh, how I loathe such impatience. Where has the art of craft and gamesmanship gone?"

"I'm going to go look for it now," Maricella said. "I'll stop by for a visit later, Damon. We've yet to discuss the Monet. Read up and we'll have a nice chat—the kind where there's actually an exchange of information as opposed to flatulent loquaciousness."

It was the verbal equivalent of sticking her tongue out at her older brother.

"I'd like that," Damon said.

"You're sweet," she said to Damon.

"Be *nice*," she said to her brother.

Twenty Three

Antonio stared silently at Damon, the only sound being the arpeggiated tap of fingers off his desk. Within him lay all the answers to Damon's questions, but he was playing it so close to the vest one would have thought he was playing a million dollar hand in Monaco.

No matter. Damon was somewhere else. And now he had the desire to be somewhere else. He took in the lay of the land, computing distances and probabilities until he formulated maps and blueprints. He feigned impatience and got up to study the Monet and the library offerings, but he was working the room like a surveyor studying a plot of land. He took a virtual tour of the house and grounds. The risks were of the usual variety. The wildcards were always the same.

People. How many, and where were they.

And these ones were probably armed.

"You have a propensity for daydreaming, Mr. Ramp, as I have learned is your want. You need to learn to be better focused," Antonio said.

Damon played along. "Oh, I'm sorry. You were saying?"

Antonio picked up the phone on the desk. It didn't ring or buzz or light up.

"I see," he said. "Continue." He hung up the phone and looked at Damon. "Perhaps an item of interest to you."

"I was hoping something would turn up eventually," Damon said.

"Turn up, indeed. Goes by the name of Hadji. So you can safely stow those thoughts of leaving you were just having. You wouldn't want anything to happen to your friend, would you?"

The wiseguy behind the dapper curtain revealed his true self. The chill in his eyes seemed to drop the temperature in the room.

"I wouldn't want anything of the nature of your implication to happen to anybody," Damon said. "But watch out for my mom—she's cagey as all get-out. She'll give Guido a run for the money. Swings a wicked handbag."

"Ah, that's more like it. Wonderful, and duly noted. As is my point, I trust?"

"Uh-huh."

"Very well then." Antonio rose from his desk. "I have affairs to attend to. I'm sure you'll be most comfortable here. Are we of an understanding?"

"We are."

Damon was undeterred by Antonio's threats and continued his assessment of his surroundings. The mob doesn't operate under any type of collective bargaining agreement and they don't negotiate. They do what they want to do, when they want to do it. Whether Damon stayed or not would have no outcome on their actions. And Hadji could take care of himself. He had probably made them before they made him. All Damon could do was wish him the best, and hope he was on his A-game.

Ain't nobody like me, Jethro.

Twenty Four

amon was running language analysis protocols of his entire conversation with Antonio and Maricella. It was a practice he called
sifting, and it was largely a search for probable clues and subtext. But
his thoughts of Maricella kept getting in the way. Damon was growing incredibly fond of her in a very short period of time. He wanted
to see her again soon. Although there was an initial physical attraction, it was highly nuanced, the feeling warmer and deeper and with
a more familial quality to it. And it was his preoccupation with her
and what she said that put him back on track.

A red flag popped.

We've yet to discuss the Monet. Read up and we'll have a nice chat...

So he did.

The Monet section of the art book was conveniently bookmarked
with a blank, unsealed white envelope. The envelope contained min-
iaturized copies of blueprints to the house and grounds and a hand-
drawn map of his immediate area. Complete with all the service
entrances and secret passageways throughout the house. There was a
drawing of two shoes in the library, initialed "L" for left and "R" for
right, like Andy Warhol's *Dance Diagram* print. A fitting art reference

from Maricella. There was a line of dashes for the shoes to follow. It was an escape map. On the bottom of the page it said: HOPE YOU HAVE ROOM FOR DESSERT. DEPART SUN 11:30 PM. Thirty-four hours to study and digest.

Damon hoped she was kidding about the dessert part.

Twenty Five

Damon went to work, curling up on the couch with the opened art book for cover. The dashes from the shoes in the library led to the right of the Monet. The service entrance. Maricella was brilliant. It were as though she was taking him by the hand. There was a small square drawn on the map, right of the Monet, at five o'clock. Damon did a virtual walk-through and imagined himself in front of the Monet, squaring himself and reaching down with his right hand to five o'clock. The release for the service entrance.

Check.

Outside the service entrance was a T. To the left was the kitchen, but the dashes went right, down a curving passageway that followed the perimeter of the house. There was another T about a hundred feet down, with stairs on both sides. There was a large square marked at the bottom of the stairs, on the left, marked "PR." *Panic room.* The stairs on the right led to another T, a set of stairs that curved around to another room marked "ARM." *Armory.* Tools of a violent trade. There was a number under the letters: 3030. *Password.* A fitting password for just such a room. And the password was there for a reason. A reason that gave Damon considerable pause.

He'll need a gun.

Opposite the armory was another set of stairs that led to a long tunnel that went underneath the house to the backyard. There was a wooded area about two hundred feet from the back of the house, leading to an escarpment. On the map, on the cusp of the wooded area, was another square marked "GARD?" *Guardhouse.* But with a bold question mark attached. The considerable pause came back. The wildcard that Damon feared most might be holed up in that guardhouse. And Maricella was telling him to grab a gun. At the bottom of the escarpment was a road. The road was unmarked, sans for the arrow pointing north. End of directions.

Check.

Considerable pause.

Zero hour Sun 23:30 CST.

Twenty Six

Dinner was beef Wellington, with scalloped potatoes and fresh green beans sautéed in olive oil with slivered garlic and almonds. It was served relatively early in terms of a usual dinner hour, perhaps due to the fact that there had been no lunch, perhaps also due to his friendly joust with Antonio. Maybe they didn't eat lunch. Maybe Maricella instructed them not to serve Damon lunch so he could study undisturbed. Dinner came courtesy of Raymond, a phlegmatic sixtyish man in formal evening wear, who went about his business in a very utilitarian manner, but when pressed was instructed to give his name, rank, and serial number, and nothing more. Damon settled for two words: "Raymond, sir." Raymond appeared via the main doors to the library, to ensure that the service entrance remained secret.

Dessert was chocolate cake and coffee, and when it was deemed that Damon had had sufficient time to dine, Raymond reappeared, to get the dishes and to offer a snifter of brandy. Damon requested a pitcher of water as well. Raymond obliged. The brandy was served warm. It had a subtle smokiness of aged oak with a note of spice. Much smoother than Old Crow.

Damon anticipated that his second dessert course might be a bit on the dry side, but it would go down easier thanks to some pleasant company. Maricella. She sat on the couch next to Damon and opened the art book, and began a dissertation on Monet, then onto Impressionism, before branching out into a general overview of art history, tearing strips of the notes she gave Damon and offering them to him, insisting that he finished his other dessert. She wasn't kidding, and the subject was non-negotiable. She kept talking until he finished.

"Any questions?"

"Just the one," Damon said, alluding to the only question mark on the intelligence he was given.

"Yes. The one," Maricella said. "Do you play poker?"

"I like Scrabble better," Damon said.

"I'll assume you're a quick study." She pulled out a deck of cards. She dealt five cards apiece. "Joker's wild."

Damon flipped over a royal flush.

"Only one hand beats a royal flush," Maricella said, getting up and walking toward the door. She left her cards face down.

Damon flipped them over after she left.

Four aces and a joker.

The one hand. Maricella had anticipated Damon's question and prepared accordingly.

The wildcard was still in play. But the message Maricella sent in metaphorically answering Damon's question did offer some reassurance.

At least she was going to try and stack the deck in his favor.

Twenty Seven

Damon dreamed of the French countryside through an Impressionistic lens, a dewy wood surrounding a pond of water lilies, an arched wooden bridge spanning a glistening brook. He had dreamt through Monet's eyes, the colors as vivid as Damon had ever seen, his mind's eye not subject to the acute red-green color blindness that had always plagued him.

The dream was suspended by a commotion in the foyer. Hushed voices accompanied by radio transmissions and the bustle of people and machinery. Damon peeked through the double doors. The foyer was filled with paramedics, a handful of guys in Italian suits, household staff, a couple of small children, and Antonio and Maricella.

And the old man, prostrate on a gurney.

The lack of urgency in everyone's movement indicated the old man's condition.

He was dead.

Maricella noticed Damon in the doorway and rushed over to see him. She had tears in her eyes and appeared harried and distraught. She whispered one word, placing it directly in his ear.

"*Move.*"

Twenty Eight

Damon paused in shock for a moment and drew a deep breath. Then his brain lit up like Time's Square on New Year's Eve.

All circuits on.

Move.

His brain was in fast-forward, ahead of his physical movement, blazing a trail for him to follow. He was in the perfect state. He didn't have to think. His brain was on cruise control. Keep your eyes open, and slow and steady wins the race. He walked over to the Monet and moved his right hand to five o'clock and pressed the panel. Open sesame. He slipped through the door and instinctively turned around and reached with his right hand to three o'clock and pressed. Close sesame. And it wasn't even on the map. His brain kicked up a notch. Cruise control clicked off. Afterburners on.

Rock 'n' roll.

He moved down the curving passageway and came to the second T, with the stairs on both sides. Moved right to the third T, and hit the stairs that curved around to the armory. Punched in *3030*. Open sesame.

Holy shit.

A room with a view. There was a wall of security monitors covering the entire grounds of the estate. Bird's-eye views. And enough armaments to overthrow most countries. Just add some rebels, instant coup. Two monitors caught Damon's eye. The foyer was still buzzing with activity. All parties still present. Then there was the guardhouse, that wildcard that stood between Damon and his freedom. There was no guard present. But there was something else in the picture. It was either fog or smoke or someone's—or something's—breath.

Damon scanned the wall of firearms, working his way down from the assault weapons to a nice assortment of handguns, in every size, shape, and caliber. He passed on the semiautomatics, because he didn't know how to rack a round into the chamber, and wasn't sure if they had safeties, and sure didn't have time for a primer. But he had seen plenty of *Dirty Harry* movies, so you go with what you know. He chose modestly from the line of revolvers. The .44 Magnums were out of stock. He settled for a Smith & Wesson .357 Magnum with a four-inch barrel, blued steel, fully loaded for his convenience.

He slid the gun in his pocket and went down the stairs that led to the long tunnel that led to the outside world. He unconsciously slowed down as he made his way through the tunnel. There was a problem. His brain was being flooded with so much information and possible scenarios that he had a system crash. His PC file was of no use. He hit a gray area. It was the great unknown.

The wildcard.

It was fear. Potential violence. He came to the outside door. Pressed his head against the cold steel in hopes that his mind would clear. It felt good but it didn't help.

He opened the door.

Twenty Nine

Seeing the proverbial light at the end of the tunnel, along with a deep breath of fresh air, allowed for a partial systems restore. Damon's geography profiles program came online, and he took in the lay of the land. The distance to the woods his GP file calculated coincided with the distance on the map. Roughly two hundred feet. But there was a variable that didn't get included in the equation.

Snow.

There was a path to the guardhouse, but it was sixty feet to the right. What lay in front of Damon was two hundred feet of snowy field. Indeterminate depth. There was another exit out of the building, and Damon considered heading back to find it. It was a short consideration. He liked the angle to the guardhouse. Better still, the angle was in the dark. The path was lit. And a frontal assault was not his strong suit. Also, foolish. Best to stay in the darkness.

Time to play Admiral Peary.

But this Admiral Peary was dressed like a salesman.

Damon plunged a tasseled loafer into the snow and went in right up to his knee, the snow following the path of least resistance, sneaking right up the inside of his pants leg. He swung his other leg around like he was trying to mount a horse. Both legs in, the tail of his navy overcoat billowed like a dress, resting on the snowpack. He buttoned up his coat and fished his gloves out of his pocket. He tightened up his tie and flipped his collars up to try to keep warm. He figured he could cover about two feet with each awkward step. It would be like mounting a horse a hundred times. One foot in, swing the leg over.

One down, ninety-nine to go.

Damon figured he could cover a full step about every five seconds. He factored in a two to five second rest between steps. Considering the distance, he weighted the calculation toward the five-second rest, a variable likely to grow longer as he progressed. Slow and steady wins the race. He didn't want to be on the verge of collapse when he reached the guardhouse. He didn't know what would be waiting for him when he arrived, but he needed some breath left to deal with the wildcard. Estimated time of arrival: Seventeen minutes.

After ten steps, Damon's calculations were confirmed. Right on schedule. After twenty, he no longer cared. He was cold and his legs were tired, the muscles on the inside of his thighs beginning to burn. He switched to a shuffling baby-steps technique for a few steps, but the snow was too densely packed, and the technique exhausting. He got back on the horse.

At the halfway point, frustration set in. Which quickly turned into an anger he was unaccustomed to feeling, but he got a bonus of determination, which would fuel the rest of his journey. He started harboring wild thoughts about what awaited him. And what he would do. He was falling into a darkness of thought, which made the anger burn a little hotter. He reached the bottom of the hole. And the proverbial fork in the road.

Fight or flight.

The considerable pause vaporized.

He was ready to fight.

Thirty

It wouldn't look cool, there would be no delivery of clever catch-phrases, and it wouldn't be clean and decisive. It would be awkward and nervous, somewhere between Barney Fife and Dirty Harry, with a pronounced list toward the Fife side of the equation. Damon hoped that the necessity of situation and a good dose of determination would at least steer him toward a Spartan utilitarianism. It didn't have to look pretty, as long as it got the job done.

A series of sixes popped in his brain unprompted. *6.6666666.* Book of Revelation allusion to the mark of the beast aside—and a blast of creepy devil music from *The Omen*—it was a calculation. He was forty feet out. *6.7 minutes,* rounding up.

Then another variable was added. An audio variable.

They were indistinct sounds at first, currents of white noise floating through the night air. Then applause. And laughter.

It was a radio.

It was Jack Benny. And the old radio jingle for Jell-O, his sponsor.

J-E-L-L . . . OHHH.

Wait, Damon thought. *How can I be hearing a radio?*

There were three windows in the small brick building, one in the back, and one on each side. The two Damon could see appeared closed and the shades or curtains were drawn. Then he went back to the picture of the guardhouse he saw on the security monitor back in the armory.

The smoke or fog was heat escaping or someone's breath.

The front door had to be open.

But the smoke or fog was no longer there, and there was no slant of light emanating from the doorway to suggest that the door was open. But it had to be. How else could he be hearing a radio?

And it was open for a long time. In the winter. Damon flashed back to the question mark in the square on the map marked "GARD?"

The one question.

Yes. The one.

He heard Maricella's voice.

Do you play poker?

Damon could see an opening to the woods in front of the guardhouse, a path that led down the escarpment. On both sides of the path were dense woods, so if Damon went straight ahead, he'd have to fight his way through the trees. In the dark. Down a steep hill. And it would be noisy. And dangerous. He would avoid a direct confrontation with whomever was in that guardhouse, but he would arouse them anyway as he tried to fight his way through the dense woods, cracking branches and crunching snow along the way.

He was going to meet the wildcard either way.

Rock and a hard place, Damon thought.

Then he had an idea, and made the choice.

He went with the rock.

A snowball.

It was time for another choice. Either hit the back window of the guardhouse with the snowball and flush whoever was in there out, or overshoot and lob one into the high trees, which would hopefully bring the guy out with his back turned. A direct shot would bring the guy out, and he would instinctively look toward the direction of the shot.

Damon packed a snowball as densely as he could, knowing he would need it to be as close as possible to a rock so it would carry into the trees. There was a stand of snow-covered pines to the right of the path, right in front of the guardhouse, so he figured a shot into the tops of the trees would shake loose a bunch of snow and make enough of a rustling noise to flush whoever was in there, out.

Damon squared himself to his target, but realized he would need the strength of his lower body and at least a few steps to carry the forty feet. He couldn't arm it that far. And he was knee-deep in snow.

He began tamping down the snow around him in order to create a launching pad that would give him a few steps and allow a good windup. He made three extra snowballs in case he missed.

His first attempt landed him flat on his back before he could even release the snowball. Tasseled loafers with leather soles were a poor substitute for baseball spikes. He took his shoes off.

His second attempt was better, but he overshot the trees by ten feet. It made a weak rustle when it landed, and Damon waited for a response. Nothing.

He shanked his third attempt left, and it made about the same sound as his first throw. Nothing.

His fourth attempt was right on the money. It had ten times the impact of his first two throws, bringing down a healthy tuft of snow and shaking loose a couple of dead branches. Damon crouched down and waited. He could still hear the radio.

Nothing. No way anyone in there could have missed that one. Damon could hear it loud and clear from forty feet away.

He put his shoes back on and got back on the horse.

Thirty One

Damon proceeded ahead in an awkward march. One foot in, swing the leg over. His energy and wind were somewhat restored, and he picked up the pace. His lower legs, and especially his feet, were ice-cold and numb. But his upper body was warm, although clammy from his expedition. The radio was loud and clear and had moved on to the next show, *The Shadow*. He was twenty feet out. He would be at the guardhouse in a few minutes. Still, nothing.

There was no welcoming party to greet him when he arrived, although he didn't exactly announce his arrival at the front door, which was, indeed, open. He paused at the side of the building and listened for signs of life.

Still nothing, except voices from the past.

And one voice silenced.

He was on his back with his legs and arms splayed, frozen in place due to the cold which hastened a rigor mortis process brought on by two gunshot wounds, one in the chest, and one in the forehead. The pool of blood was partially frozen. The semiautomatic was half out of its shoulder holster.

He was too late.

Damon stood in the doorway and gave into the shock for a moment. It wasn't a conscious choice. His systems went silent. There was no thought. Just the stillness of death. The same feeling he had when he saw Harry at the drugstore. Then Damon turned and looked at the path in front of the building, that descended down into the dark woods.

Move.

It was a forty-five-degree incline down the escarpment, and the path that was suggested by the opening into the woods narrowed within about ten feet to no path at all. There were sporadic openings that suggested that maybe someone had walked through there at one time, but nature had mostly closed the gap.

Walking forward was awkward, so Damon started using a side-stepping technique, planting a right foot down the hill, then bringing in his left to join his right. No road in sight. Just pines and low-hanging poplars and birches, which he pushed away with his right arm as he stepped, which he had to keep upright and extended to keep from getting whacked in the face by low-hanging branches.

There were no footsteps to follow. There also were no footsteps to follow across the snowy field to the guardhouse. Damon concluded that whoever snuffed that guard had to have come up the path to the guardhouse. There was a back window to the building, probably a security camera, so anyone coming up that path would easily have been spotted. Damon didn't need to fire up his PC file for this one.

The guard had to have known his assailant.

It was an inside job.

Thirty Two

Although his glasses protected his eyes, Damon's arm was losing the battle of the brush. The woods grew thicker as he progressed, and nothing short of a shield would have kept his face from getting scratched. And he was being scratched badly. His raw wounds were stinging, being clawed repeatedly by the barbs of cold branches. He was fully engulfed in pain, head to toe, inside and out. But another audio variable brushed his pain aside.

It was a car.

Damon stilled himself to tune into the sound, determining direction, recalibrating his bearings. He saw a flash of headlights, which allowed him a glimpse of his destination. Another fifty feet and he would be on the road.

Chalk up another one for Admiral Peary.

Damon placed a snow-encrusted loafer on the asphalt. Then another. He stomped his feet to get the snow off, but it didn't help. Most of the snow was on the inside. And it hurt. His face hurt. As did his quadriceps, hamstrings, triceps, and deltoids. And he had a screaming headache to boot.

But there was a car waiting.

It was a dark sedan, and it was parked on the side of the unlit S-shaped road, about ninety feet up. It was running, its lights dark. Then the brake lights lit up. It was an Audi. Then again. A blue Audi. Two flashes. Then the reverse lights came on, lighting a path for Damon to follow. Someone was expecting him. Then another audio.

"Damon!"

It was Maricella.

It was a long ninety feet. Damon broke into a jog to hasten the final leg of his journey, but the hard surface kicking back at his frozen feet put a halt to that idea. He winced with every step. Rare combinations of words emanated from his mouth in concert with each movement. Bad words unaccustomed by such a delicate palate. Damon's voice lacked the punch to deliver a good blue streak. It had all the toughness of a little boy asking his mom to pass the potatoes.

Damon once again basked in the warmth and smell of fine leather, made even sweeter by the smell of Maricella. She turned the heater up high before pulling away.

"Are you okay?" she said.

"I think so," Damon said, pulling his shoes and socks off. He checked his face in the visor mirror. It looked like a cat had used it for a scratching post. Maricella turned on one of the interior lights to see for herself.

"I'll stop when I can," she said. "But it's going to be a while. We need to get moving."

"Where are we going?" Damon asked.

"You're going home—well, maybe not exactly home," Maricella said. "But we'll find a place. I'm coming with you."

"I'm sorry about your father," Damon said.

"He's your father, too, Damon."

Maricella looked at Damon to gauge his reaction. The scratches on his face were more interesting than his reaction.

"I know," Damon said. "But he's more your father than mine.

He's nothing but a stranger to me, just an old man. And that makes you my sister."

"Welcome to the family."

"And what's going on with our family, Maricella? There's a dead man back at the guardhouse."

"There's two more in the house. Maybe more by now," Maricella said.

"What's happening?"

"You know how there's hostile takeovers of corporations? Well, they don't come any more hostile than the kind of takeovers that happen in family business. Our father was murdered—probably poisoned. And they tried to kill Antonio."

"Someone on the inside?"

"That's how it usually goes."

"Was the purpose of my kidnapping simply to fulfill a dying father's wish?"

"In part, yes. But I'm sure Antonio had ulterior motives as well. As to what, I have no idea. People who interfere with family interests usually go away. You need to be careful where you stick that cute little nose."

"How much do you know about the family business? What I stumbled onto is pretty disturbing."

"It's all disturbing. It always has been and always will be. It's about making a living off the exploitation of others, the destruction of human lives. True blood money. As far as the particulars of our family's interests, I couldn't say. What exactly did you stumble onto?"

"High-end blackmail and male prostitution involving minors. It's all run out of a small flower shop, slash adult novelty store, in St. Paul. The back rooms of the place are wired. But there's a beehive of activity surrounding it. The feds got it staked out and there's some independent contractors at work, looking for a piece of the action. But some of them are plants, chumming the waters, looking for the big fish."

"Sounds like the usual specialties. And you got involved in this how?"

"I tried to sell them yellow pages advertising."

"Seriously?"

"Seriously."

"No kidding?"

"No kidding—and you better let that laugh out before your eyes pop out of your head."

All the way to Hinckley.

Thirty Three

Maricella needed the laugh. It was long and cathartic and contagious. Damon needed it, too. If only it didn't hurt so damn much.

The tears came when she was alone, like they always do. They visited her while she was waiting for Damon outside a wayside rest. She tried to hide it at first, like people always do. As if they were the only ones who ever cried.

Damon lent his new sister his shoulder for a moment before they hit the road. It was another new feeling for Damon, another he was unaccustomed to, but liked very much. The feeling had a similar warmth to the one he felt when Milah addressed him by all her pet names. It made him feel warm and liked. *Milah.*

The closer they got to the Twin Cities the more Damon's brain reengaged to previous matters, after his unexpected respite somewhere in the hills of Duluth. Back at the fore were Milah and Burl, Mom's USS *Lincoln*, assorted WDMs, and his favorite fisher of men, Rumples. But most of all, it was about Hadji. He was in about as tough a spot as they come. Damon asked Maricella for a cell phone, but she didn't have one. Of course. Cell phones can be tracked. No cell phone family plans for these types of family members. Come to think of it, they don't care much for the landline variety either. They can be tapped. Most family business was conducted face to face. Better yet, mouth to ear. Whispered. With a hand covering their mouth so no one could read their lips. Wiseguys.

Hadji would have to wait. The Twin Cities were an hour away. Damon hoped that Maricella could be a little more helpful with his next query. Pretty basic stuff.

"What's my real name?"

"You were born Damonico Aloicious Naimo, firstborn of Giuseppe and Elisabetta Naimo, August 20, 1964."

"And now for the million dollar question."

"This might take a while," Maricella said, "and I don't have all the details of what happened. You were born at a very volatile time in family history."

"You don't ever say the word, do you?" Damon asked.

"Habit."

"Just for the record," Damon said, "you are referring to Mafia history, are you not?"

"Especially not for the record."

"Touché."

"There was a lot of volatility and pressure on all the families, from all sides, in the sixties," Maricella said. "There was a lot of infighting going on, a lot of mistrust, power was being consolidated and people were being moved out. And on top of it all, there was a lot of heat from the government, from Kefauver to Kennedy to Joe Valachi—all culminating in the Banana War."

"The Joseph Bonanno kidnapping?"

"October 1964. There were other kidnapping threats and attempts as well."

"Involving our family?"

"You were born in the eye of a hurricane," Maricella said. "There were threats."

"I was moved for safekeeping? And here I thought there was an honor code among families—that innocent children were off-limits."

"It got really nasty," Maricella said. "There were a lot of new players in the mix, too—thanks mostly to the drug trade, which turned into this huge, unwieldy monster, just like the old-timers said it would."

"And suddenly it was no-holds-barred."

"Everyone became a goldfish in the piranha tank."

"Well, that's half the equation," Damon said. "I suspect the second half will be a little harder to come by."

"The real million dollar question is why you never came back," Maricella said. "And that, I'm afraid, I don't have the answer to. I'm sorry, Damon."

"There are answers for every question ever posited by humankind," Damon said. "Some are just harder than others."

Thirty Four

Damon's rationalist aside silenced both him and Maricella. All that could be heard was the hum of fine Teutonic automobile engineering, a taut purr in which to ponder all life's questions.

They had a lot of them.

Maricella got the ball rolling. Best to start with the simple ones.

"Where to?" she said, pointing to the sign of many choices, St. Paul or Minneapolis.

Damon was still lost in the hum. The Great Damonico, ponderer of the great mysteries of life. He even had himself in a black cape. With a crazy Daliesque mustache.

It made him laugh.

"Damon?"

"I'm sorry. What?"

"Were you in your happy fun place?" Maricella said.

"Kind of."

"Do you do that often?"

"I kind of go away sometimes."

"Ah, a nice segue back to my question," Maricella said. "Speaking of going away, where to, St. Paul or Minneapolis?"

"Do you think it matters, safetywise? Is anyone going to come looking for you?"

"Not likely. The real danger was back around the house. That's why we had to get moving—I wasn't sure who was lurking around the neighborhood. I'm family, yes, but I'm also a civilian. And safetywise doesn't matter, because if they want to find you, they find you. There is nowhere in the world you can hide that they can't get to."

"Again, not saying the word. You were trained well," Damon said.

"Again, habit."

"Did you just mock me?"

"I think I did."

"Well, that didn't take long. You've been my sister for five minutes and you're already giving me guff."

"Guff?"

"Sass."

"Sass? Again, not saying the word," Maricella said.

"I don't swear," Damon said.

"Coulda swore I heard some effenheimers back on the road when I picked you up."

"Only when I'm hiking."

"So are we hiking to St. Paul or Minneapolis?"

"St. Paul's home," Damon said.

"Then St. Paul's home," Maricella said. "But just so you know, I'm going shopping in Minneapolis." She looked over Damon's clothes. "Perhaps you should come with me. There's some fine men's shops across the river, you know. I'm buying."

"That's right, you're rich."

"Membership has its privileges."

"Staying at my place would probably be a bad idea," Damon said. "Considering the last two times I was there I was kidnapped."

"Who grabbed you the first time?"

"The feds."

"Why?"

"To protect me from the guys who grabbed me the second time."

"That's not very good protecting," Maricella said.

"No, it's not. Actually, I was being gift-wrapped for the second party. Free delivery, too. Got a neat used car to boot."

"Nice. But a bit ham-handed, don'tcha think?"

"More like ham-brained, but they took a whack at it."

"Swing and a miss," Maricella said. "They probably changed cars five times."

"I only remember the one."

"One more than most."

Maricella pointed at the St. Paul skyline, the familiar 1st of the First National Bank building flashing on the horizon.

"Hotel San Pablo okay?" she said.

It was Damon's favorite part of the city. Rice Park. The Ordway. Landmark Center. The Romanesque stature of the St. Paul Central Library.

"Okay," Damon said.

Thirty Five

The Hotel San Pablo was unaccustomed to check-ins at two-thirty in the morning, and Maricella was told as much when she asked for a room. But the smug indignance of an assistant concierge stuck on the night shift was no match for the dignified grace and gravitas of someone like Maricella, who without raising her voice or voicing complaint, procured a suite within thirty seconds of Caleb's initial bout of smug, who suddenly, miraculously, couldn't do enough for her. Of course it didn't hurt that she gave Caleb a lovely pocket square made out of a crisp fifty dollar bill and laid down an American Express Platinum card to cover expenses. Maricella also suggested that she and Damon might be hungry, and that she would be calling him shortly to fetch them some food. Caleb nodded politely and addressed her forthwith as "ma'am."

The room and the view were spectacular, and the beds and couches and chairs and blankets were all thick and plush. But of more importance to Damon was the bathroom, and the promise of a hot shower or bath and nice soft towels and maybe some pain relievers. And it had a deep whirlpool bath. Damon told Maricella he would be going away for a while.

When Damon came back a half hour later there was food waiting. Maricella had put Caleb to work as she said she would, and there was a smorgasbord of greasy delights from Mickey's Diner. Bacon, sausage, pancakes, eggs, mounds of hash browns, and a couple of sandwiches and burgers, just in case. Maricella took her turn in the bathroom and came back out to join her brother. They both were wearing white terrycloth robes of very high thread counts. They raised their LDL levels.

"Thank you, Maricella," Damon said. "You know how to roll, sister."

"That I do. And you're welcome."

"I'm guessing you figured this out already, but I'm kind of poor. I can't afford any of this. I'm afraid I'm a not-so-good salesman working in a not-so-good industry that's about a foot away from the grave."

"You are no longer poor," Maricella said. "You're family and are entitled to all family privileges. Probably entitled to some kind of back pay. Think of all the generous allowances you missed out on."

"And pinky rings and sharkskin suits."

"So there is a sense of humor under there."

"I think it's stress related," Damon said. "I guess being kidnapped and being tortured by mean branches did something to me. And I've never seen a gangland murder victim before."

"How many gangland murder witnesses does it take to screw in a lightbulb?"

"Honestly, a joke? First sass, now jokes."

"You're wrecking my joke. How many gangland murder witnesses does it take to screw in a lightbulb?"

"I don't know. How many?"

"What lightbulb?"

"Keep the day job," Damon said.

"My day job is being rich, and I have no intention whatsoever of giving it up. In fact, you should take tomorrow off and come to work with me. We've business to transact. And it's a cute joke."

"That's a thought. A very good thought. Perhaps you can come to work with me as well. See one of our family's operations up close and personal."

"Can we do a stakeout? I want to play private eye."

"We could," Damon said. "You might recognize some faces."

"I might," Maricella said. "And I might be able to give you an insider's view of what's happening. Tricks of the trade, so to speak."

"See things in a whole new light," Damon said.

"Want to hear another joke? I like lightbulb jokes."

"My Cosa Nostra sister, the comedienne."

Thirty Six

Sunday morning was bright and mild, and Damon and Maricella enjoyed the late AM hours at a sunny window table at the San Grille, brunching on corned beef hash and Bloody Marys. It was Damon's first Bloody Mary, and Maricella made sure it was done right, requesting top-shelf pepper vodka and bottles of Worcestershire and Tabasco sauces, so she could doctor their concoctions just right. Like everything else with Maricella, they were. She also had a way of getting right to the point.

"Show me the flower shop," she said.

"Are we playing private eye now?"

"We are. And I want to play now."

"Did you want to stop at Macy's and pick up a trench coat and a fedora?" Damon said.

"Tomorrow, shop. Today, play private eye."

"Okay, Tonto."

"Again with the humor," Maricella said. "There's hope for you yet, Damon Ramp. What else do you have up your sleeve?" She looked over his clothes again. "Those poor, unfortunate, threadbare sleeves—you're coming shopping with me tomorrow."

"Yes, Tonto."

Damon guided Maricella uptown, where they did a drive-by past Petal to the Metal. They settled into the spot that Damon had previously occupied, give or take a car or two, and Damon pointed out all the particulars around the shop. Rumples wasn't at his usual post, there was no activity in the windows of the School Book Depository, and no strange choreography of traffic on the sidewalks or ten-year-olds lurking in the bushes that surrounded the shop. Maricella produced a small rectangular box from her purse. She snapped open a pair of compact binoculars.

"Played private eye before, have you?" Damon said.

"They come in handy," Maricella said. She scanned the scene briefly. "We have company."

"Where?"

"In the used car lot. Blue Buick."

Damon took a look for himself.

"Well, whaddaya know," he said. "Rumples got himself a new car."

"Meet Special Agent William Charles, FBI."

"You know him?"

"We've met," Maricella said. "He's been sniffing around our family since the late seventies. He is the absolute personification of persistence."

"The man is diligent. Thanks, sister. Had a feeling you might come in handy."

"There's more to this than just blackmail and prostitution. Charles was DEA before he went to the Bureau. He brought his skill set with him to his new job."

"Are you saying there's drugs involved in this, too?"

"Multitiered business models are hardly a new concept in family business. They're very efficient, you know. They squeeze their dollars, just like Walmart."

"Eyes on the prize."

"Hmm?"

"Just something I once said," Damon said.

"There's something else you should know, too."

"What's that?"

"That this whole thing is a helluva lot more dangerous than you thought it was. Still want to play?"

Damon gulped.

"Damn straight," she said.

Thirty Seven

Maricella said she had her first encounter with Special Agent William Charles when she was eleven, in 1980. But the memory mostly revolved around her father, back when he was at the zenith of his power and vitality. She said her father seemed more amused than worried by the overzealous G-man, who was trying to make a name for himself through sheer force of will, a real go-getter. She wanted to carry on the family tradition of amusement.

"Wanna take a walk?" Maricella said. "Let's see if we can get Eliot Ness some exercise."

Damon smiled. He liked her spunky attitude. And Hadji called him that, too.

"I don't think Rumples is the walking type," Damon said. "At least he doesn't leave the car much. He's no spring chicken, you know."

"Rumples?" Maricella said.

"It was the first word that came to mind when I first saw him. He had on a rumpled trench coat over a rumpled navy suit. Even his face seemed rumpled. His character too. He's just a rumply man."

"Well, the rumpled old chicken is about to fly the coop," Maricella said. "Shall we?"

She led Damon down the sidewalk toward the corner, stopping at the crosswalk across from the used car lot. It was a bold call right out of Rumples's playbook. Human bait reverse on two.

Hut hut.

Rumples sprang from his car like a teenage boy going to the house where his girlfriend was babysitting. Maricella and Damon crossed the street. Rumples took full advantage of the pedestrian right-of-way laws, still a dicey proposition on a busy Grand Avenue, charging across the street. The three arrived on the opposite corner at the same time.

"My oh my, has the plot just thickened," Rumples said. "Hello, Miss Naimo, nice to see you again. And Mr. Ramp. I hardly know where to begin."

"Special Agent Charles, what a nice surprise," Maricella said. "What brings you to the Saintly City?"

"My exact question to you, young lady," Rumples said. "Have a little trouble up north?"

"Oh, just a little dustup. Cost of doing business," Maricella said.

"You're more like your father than Antonio is," Rumples said. "An absolute ice-cold martini. Speaking of Antonio, is he knocking about the city as well? I'd love to see him."

"Wouldn't you now. I am not my brother's keeper, Secret Agent Charles. And I much prefer Grey Goose martinis."

"Cheeky," Rumples said. "Boys go to the mattresses yet?"

"You've seen too many movies," she said.

"Your brother got greedy," Rumples said. "Ruffled the wrong feathers. Hate to be in his shoes."

Maricella looked at Rumples's shoes. "Actually, you would love to be in his shoes. Still shopping at Sears, are you?"

"Again with the cheeky. And Mr. Ramp—have a little trouble with a cat, did you?"

"Mean branches," Damon said.

"Oh God, not another one." Rumples nodded at Maricella.

"You've been hanging around this one a little too long. Enjoying the family reunion?"

"Am I to thank you for finally bringing us together?" Damon said.

"Beats selling yellow pages advertising, doesn't it? Which, I might add, you're not very good at."

"Where have I heard that one before?" Damon said.

Rumples smiled. "So, how are we going to play this? Obstruction of justice for two, perhaps?"

"Do you know the eighties' Bobby Brown hit that is germane to this situation?" Maricella said to Rumples. "Oh, of course you don't. Come, Damon, let's go shopping."

Maricella took Damon by the hand and led him down the sidewalk toward Petal to the Metal. Rumples put his hands on his hips and watched them walk away.

"Oh, Miss Naimo?" Rumples said. "I *do*. Goddam right it's my prerogative. Tell Antonio I said hello. Oh, never mind, I'll just tell him myself at the funeral."

"Please try to look presentable," Maricella said. "Iron your shirt. Perhaps wear an iron shirt."

"Cheeky."

Thirty Eight

A dark-skinned man in a dark blue suit exited Milah's and changed Maricella's mind about shopping. She tugged Damon around in an abrupt about-face, hurrying him down the sidewalk and around the corner, wordless and tense. Two cameras came up and began shooting, one from the passenger side of a charcoal SUV parked down from Rumples in the used car lot, and one up on the third floor of the School Book Depository. Damon's internal databases popped to life with the flash of information. VF and PC files tagged him as an Afghan or a Turk, given their countries' collective proclivity toward the drug trade, matched with relevant details germane to the current situation. And the look was right. The man was important and had import, with multiple interested parties. He was well-dressed, but he was no WDM.

Maricella pulled Damon into the nearest safe harbor, a bridal shop on Grand.

"There are laws against this, sister," Damon said.

"Now who's being the comedian?"

"Did you see the cameras?"

"I counted three."

"I made the SUV and the School Book Depository, where was the third?" Damon said.

"The what?"

"Oh, sorry—it's just how I remember things. I assign everything with the first name or description that pops into my head. Simple memory device," Damon said. "The building behind the used car lot."

"You're wonderfully silly, Damon."

"And you have the eyes of an eagle. Where was the third?"

"Right behind my car," Maricella said.

"Ruh roh."

"Did you just say 'ruh roh'?"

"I did."

"What has gotten into you?"

"Mean branches."

"Did you go through the *Wizard of Oz* forest or something? Were they grumpy apple trees?"

"What just happened here, Maricella? Who was that guy?"

"Probably the guy behind what just happened up north. Remember what Charles said about Antonio getting greedy and ruffling the wrong feathers? Likely that's the bird he was talking about."

"What's his name and what's his connection to Antonio?"

"He's known by the name of Pashtun and he's a direct link to the poppy trade in Afghanistan," Maricella said. "Knowing Antonio, he went straight to the source; he hates the middleman. I've seen and heard of him before, some of it unbelievably horrific. That tribal stuff is ruthless, and when things go south, it gets really bad. And judging by all that's happened, something definitely went south. And Pashtun was not known for his loyalty. He does business with others as well. And that's a big, big problem in family business. Loyalty and exclusivity are pillars of the code. This thing could be bad in multiple directions."

"If a guy that powerful is doing business directly in Petal to the Metal, then Petal is a major hub in the operation," Damon said.

"Twin Cities for sure, but I'm guessing the whole Midwest, at least west of Chicago." *Definitely Chicago* "Oh my…"

"'Oh my' what?"

"'Oh my' Rumples has Chicago all over him. Was he based there?"

"They have field offices all over, but yeah, a lot of business—above board and under—stems from Chicago. So?"

"So this here is more important than Chicago, right?" Damon said. "Why else would he be here?"

"Oh my."

"My point exactly," Damon said. "How big is this thing?"

Thirty Nine

A petite young woman in a black pantsuit came out from behind the counter at the bridal shop and approached Damon and Maricella. Despite her back being turned to the approaching clerk, Maricella still knew she was coming. Damon noted no reflection in the glass, and the clerk's approach was silent as she was wearing soft-soled flats. Damon was impressed by how acutely aware and observant Maricella was. Although Damon shared these gifts as well, his were more cerebrally based, affectations of a highly tuned mind. Maricella's had more of a street edge, rock-solid instincts that only nurture could provide. A lifetime of trained awareness.

More like your father than Antonio is.

Rumples was right. But so was Mrs. Gump about chocolates.

"Excuse me, are you Damon Ramp?" the clerk asked.

"Yes?" It somehow came out with a question mark attached.

"You have a phone call."

"I do?" Again with the question mark.

"No, I'm just messin' with you," the clerk said. Exasperated eye roll and heavy sarcasm.

Damon paused.

All circuits on. The heavenly warmth of neurotransmission.

"Ahem," the clerk said. "Sometime today?"

"Sorry," Damon said. He followed the clerk.

"Trouble with your cat or something?" the clerk said.

"Mean branches."

"Sure it's not cat scratch fever?"

"Bear with him," Maricella said. "He's had a rough couple of days."

"Thanks for spreading it around," the clerk said.

"Cheeky little thing," Maricella said.

Damon picked up the phone.

"Hello?"

No answer.

"Hello?" he said again.

"'Bout time you chimed in, Jethro."

Forty

"Hadji?"

"The one and only, homes. Who's the number you hangin' with?"

"The what?"

"The dish, the babe, try and keep up, Jethro. WTF, man."

"Are you okay?" Damon asked.

"Right as rain, homes. Ya gonna share or we gonna do-si-do some more?"

"That's Maricella. She's my sister."

"Get out. How'd that happen?"

"Long story."

"Lotta that goin' on," Hadji said. "Think we aimed a little low, Jethro. This thing's got more layers than a fucking wedding cake. Guido's been chasin' my ass all over the place. Eliot Ness show you a good time?"

"Guido, too," Damon said. "Took me for a ride up to the North Shore."

"Cello a souvenir?"

"It's Maricella."

"Whatev. She's got nice wheels. Cool car, too."

"Physiology is truly amazing," Damon said. "Hormones trump everything."

"Indubitably. Heh-heh."

"You're nothing but a perspicacious alley cat."

"Damn, there you go again. Hey, speaking of which—"

"Don't say it."

"Oh, I'm gonna say it, Jethro—what up with your face? Run into a bobcat up north or something?"

"The more imperative question is how did you get a look at my face?" Damon said.

"Been busy, homes," Hadji said. "Put some of my peeps to work. I got this scene wired to the rafters. Got one of my pigeons to do up the inside, too. You won't believe what I got to show you. Eliot Ness sees this, he gonna shit."

"Ahem," Maricella interrupted. "Who on God's green earth are you talking to?"

"Hey, is that the dish?" Hadji said. "Put her on, Jethro."

Damon handed Maricella the phone.

"Hello?"

"Hey, sweets—whatcha doin' with my boy, Jethro?"

"Excuse me?"

"Oh, c'mon, Cello, don't be shy. Throw a little my way, toots. Heh-heh."

"You're an insolent little demon, aren't you?" Maricella said.

"Indubitably," Hadji said. "Man, you must be my homes' sister—all this highfalutin yakkity-yak. What say you ditch Jethro and we paint up the town, sis."

Maricella handed the phone back to Damon.

"What *is* that?" she said.

"That's a Hadji," Damon said.

"Good grief."

"Ahem," the clerk interrupted. "Do you mind? We'd like to do a little business here."

"Gotta go, Hadji," Damon said. "We're at the San Pablo."

"Roger that."

"You mean I actually have to meet this creature?" Maricella said.

"You do."

"Perhaps teach him some manners."

"Building a ladder to heaven would be easier."

"Excuse me, miss," Damon said to the clerk. "My sincerest apologies for all the trouble. But, if I may, perhaps one more inconvenience?"

She rolled her eyes again and tapped her French tips off the glass counter.

"May we call a cab, please?"

"Daybed in back if you need a nap," she said. "Fix you a sandwich?" She held up her smartphone. "Ever see one of these?"

"Cheeky little thing," Maricella said.

Maricella handed the clerk a fifty.

"Better?"

"All better," the clerk said.

"Works every time, doesn't it?" Damon said.

"Makes the world go round."

Forty One

Damon and Maricella waited for Hadji at the bar of the San Grille. They were as quiet as the room was on a three o'clock Sunday afternoon, playing with their coffee cups more than they were drinking out of them. The bartender kept sneaking looks at Damon's face when he wasn't sneaking looks at Maricella, but eventually Maricella's proved more interesting, for obvious reasons. But you cannot discount the power and attraction of facial wounds. Think Jack Nicholson in *Chinatown*. What's the first thing people remember? The big honking bandage on his nose, that's what.

"Excuse me, are you Damon Ramp?" the bartender asked.

Damon nodded, no question marks attached.

"Phone call, sir." He handed Damon the phone.

"Hello?"

No answer.

"Hello?"

There was one young agitated voice and one very polite baritone voice with a slight Jamaican accent coming over the speaker. The young agitated voice just called the very polite baritone voice Jiminy Cricket.

"Excuse me," Damon said. He put down the phone.

Damon walked to the main entrance to get Hadji.

"'Bout time you got here, Jethro. Jiminy Cricket here won't let me through. Vouch."

"Is the young sir with you, sir?" the doorman asked Damon. He was wearing a top hat and tails with a red vest. *Hmph. Jiminy Cricket,* Damon thought. Except large and black with a thick goatee and a Rasta accent.

"He is."

The doorman lowered his large hand to let Hadji pass. Damon raised his to stop him.

"I believe the young sir owes the very polite doorman an apology for all the trouble," Damon said.

"Most kind of you, sir," the doorman said. "It is our burden to teach the young squires of the world, is it not?"

"What, suddenly you're my dad, homes? Hadji said. "Awright, awright. Sorry, Jim. Won't happen again."

The doorman held up his hands and said, "We are good."

"Thank you," Damon said.

"C'mon, snappity, homes. Where's the dish?"

"You need an off switch."

"Cello do all this?" Hadji said, as he and Damon took in the lobby of the hotel on their way to the Grille.

"A suite, too," Damon said. "Penthouse was taken."

"Speaking of pussy, heh-heh," Hadji said. "What up with the gnarly face?" He stopped Damon to get a closer look. "Jiminy bleeps, homes. Damn, that crazy shit. Bad fucking kitty."

"Good of you to notice."

"Indubitably."

Hadji spotted Maricella at the bar and beelined right to her. Without raising her head or looking in his direction, she put out the stop sign. Then she held up her left index finger. Class was now in session.

"Ground rules," Maricella said. "First, don't ever call me 'toots,' 'sweets,' or 'sis,' understand?"

"I'll do anything for you, doll."

"Or 'doll.'"

"Hey, garçon," Hadji called out to the bartender. "Score a Red Bull here, dude."

Maricella held up her right index finger to stop the bartender.

"And you need another stimulant about as much as that bartender needs to hear the word 'garçon' again," Maricella said.

"Been up for three, sis. Need to wind," Hadji said.

"You mean, since three?" Maricella said. "Ahem. Sis?"

"Look. I been up for three days, Cello," Hadji said. "Not really up for the hassle,'kay? So I'm gonna score a Red and show you and Jethro what I got, copacetic? Still with us, Jethro?"

"I really enjoyed that," Damon said.

"That's my boy," Hadji said. "Cello?"

"Fine," Maricella said. "But we're not finished, *capiche*?"

"Yeah, yeah, I hear ya, Cello. I be nice."

"*Please.* It's Mari—oh, never mind. Who's chasing you?"

Hadji looked at Maricella and smiled.

"Maybe someone you know, sis."

Forty Two

Hadji took a long pull off his Red Bull and fired up his laptop on the coffee table. He tapped out a flurry of keystrokes and had an image up on the screen before Maricella and Damon could join him on the couch.

"Check this guy," Hadji said.

"Pashtun," Maricella said.

"Seen this guy twice now," Hadji said. "He doesn't do anything except talk to the goth babe, but this guy just *looks* important, know what I mean? Sketchy as all get-out."

"And you're not going to see him do anything—ever," Maricella said. "Pashtun is as ice-cold as they come. He always acts like he's under surveillance, which, believe me, is a good chunk of the time. Even when there's no chance of him being recorded. He never gives anything away. He contracts out all drops and money exchanges. He uses people like soccer moms and grocery clerks and garbagemen. And the feds can't arrest you for talking unless you say something stupid."

"Sketchy's in the pharmaceutical business," Hadji said. "He sure ain't a trench-coated creeper trying to snag spring chickens—like this guy."

Hadji called up another image.

"Oh no," Damon said.

"Oh yeah, Jethro. Meet your local anchorman," Hadji said.

"And the chairman of Second Chance, the troubled youth organization," Maricella said. "God, not another one."

"Hadji?" Damon said. It had a parental tone.

Hadji received loud and clear.

"What?" Hadji said. "What difference does it make if I take him down or the cops do? He stops creepin' either way, right? C'mon, homes, this guy's my fucking retirement plan. Yummy fresh pigeon. Stop with the dad shit, already."

Hadji winked at Damon and snickered. He called up another image.

"And this guy. Straight out of central casting for the next Scorsese mob movie."

"As I live and breathe," Maricella said. "Jimmy Irish. Runs the drug end for the Collozzo family. This is bad."

"Rival family?" Damon said.

"Makes the Hatfields and McCoys look like a bridge club rivalry," Maricella said.

"Pashtun's playing both ends against the middle," Damon said.

"He's been known," Maricella said.

"How come no one caps him?" Hadji said.

"Because he's a direct link to the poppy trade in Afghanistan," Maricella said. "He's incredibly valuable—he cuts out a whole bunch of middlemen. Less slices of the pie to divvy up. And no one wants to mess with that tribal stuff."

Damon looked intensely at the picture. Upper right corner. All circuits on. The heavenly warmth of neurotransmission.

"Do you have this on a stream, Hadji?"

"Yeah," Hadji said.

"Play it," Damon said.

Hadji called up the stream.

"Watch the upper right corner," Damon said.

"What?" Maricella said.

Nothing.

"Wait," Damon said.

A heavily obstructed image of a man flashed across the upper right corner. He was in three pieces in the image.

"There," Damon said.

"You seein' things, homes," Hadji said.

"I don't see it either," Maricella said.

"Play it again and freeze it when I say 'stop.'" Damon said. "Can you reconfigure the image, get a different angle?"

"Negative," Hadji said.

He played it again.

"Stop," Damon said. He picked up a pen to use as a pointer, circling the portion of the image as he made his point. "Here's the top of his head...the waistband of what look to be gray coveralls...and doesn't that look like the wheel and the bar of a hand truck? When was this taken?"

"This morning," Hadji said.

"Odd getting a delivery on a Sunday morning, isn't it?" Damon said. "I mean, it's a flower shop and an adult novelty store, right? What, did they need an urgent delivery of lilies or leather bustiers?"

"Odd, indeed," Maricella said. "Present company considered, most decidedly odd. Whatever could be in those boxes?"

"Probably enough smack to light up a million junkies," Hadji said.

"Hadji, do you have any of the interior rooms wired?" Damon asked.

"Just the one," Hadji said. "Pretty twisted shit—wanna see?"

"There's storage in one of the adjacent rooms," Damon said. "Can you get another camera in there?"

"You asking me to use one of my pigeons, dad?"

"I wish I wasn't, but it sure would be nice to get a look in that storeroom, wouldn't it? And like you said, baldy keeps throwing you out of the store."

"Kinda moral dilemma, ain't it, Jethro?"

"It is."

"Just sayin'."

"You two all wrapped up with your father-son moment now?" Maricella said. "I'd like to see some more pictures."

"I'd do what she says," Damon said.

"Kinda figurin' that out," Hadji said. "Okay, I flagged one more guy who looked interesting. Actually, it's a twofer, cuz one guy does the talking and the other just whispers in the guy's ear."

Hadji called up the stream.

Silent film.

"Interpreter," Damon said. "Italian?"

"Sicilian," Maricella said.

"Know him?" Damon asked.

"*Diavolo Nero.*"

"Italian's a little rusty, sis," Hadji said.

"The Black Devil."

"A hit man?" Damon said.

"Probably the most lethal man in the world."

"Maybe the one dude who could take a run at Pashtun?" Hadji said. "Question is, who'd have the stones and connections to import this guy?"

"Anyone we know, sis?" Damon asked.

"I think we just went to Defcon 4," Maricella said.

Forty Three

Dinner was bourbon pork chops with apple sauce, with sides of mashed potatoes and asparagus spears in a hollandaise sauce. A Chardonnay was recommended, but Maricella insisted on a Cabernet Sauvignon, the cost of which was more than Damon had amassed in commissions in the last two weeks. Maricella saw him looking at the wine list. Damon wasn't comparing vintages.

"Would you have preferred I went with a different region Cabernet?" Maricella said.

Damon appreciated the soft manner in which she broke the ice.

"Although I'm not exactly sure how it's supposed to feel," Damon said, "I think I feel like a kept man. But it's weirder because you're my sister. And then there's the family thing..."

"Very good. Notice how you didn't say the word. You're a quick study. And it's all okay—the weird feelings, guilt, whatever you want to call it. If it's just a money thing, well, we're just calling it allowance back pay. Is it something else?"

"Moral dilemmas."

"Such as?"

"What Hadji does. What I *asked* Hadji to do. What our family does—the difference between an honest living and living off blood money. Do you ever feel guilty about any of this?"

"When I was in college I used to work as a waitress," Maricella said. "It was largely an act of defiance. All my friends were working their way through school, so I thought I should do the same. I was studying philosophy, struggling with Kant, Mill, Aristotle—getting stoned and reading Kerouac, you know, that whole getting down with the people kind of thing. So yes, I know guilt."

"You sure don't act like someone who's racked with guilt. Philosophically, where did you land?"

"I am not naïve," Maricella said. "I am very much a pragmatist and a realist, and I know exactly where the family fortune came from. Philosophically speaking, you might say I landed closest to Mill's camp—to try and do the greatest good for the greatest number. So instead of guilt I turned to philanthropy, all anonymous, of course. A lot of people get fed and clothed and sheltered and educated with that money. Blood money? Yeah, sure there's that. But by and large it's sharks going after other sharks."

"My Cosa Nostra sister, the utilitarian. Of course, you know, there are large ethical holes in your philosophy. Little bit of denial in there as well."

"Am I to assume that you are going to set me right?"

"Just sayin'."

"You and Hadji are the strangest, most disparate pairing of human beings I have ever encountered. He's rubbing off on you. But the connection is undeniable. He respects you. And you worry about him."

"I do."

"You worry about a lot of things."

"I do."

"Perhaps I can help you with that."

"Be like Mike?"

"Something like that."

"I think I'm going to quit my job," Damon said.

"My story inspired you."

"I think *you* did."

"You just earned a raise to your allowance."

"Hot diggity."

"Mean branches?"

"You have no idea."

Forty Four

Monday morning started with a phone call for Damon. It was a brief call.

"Are they going to miss you?" Maricella asked.

"Only in a sarcastic manner. 'How will we ever press on without you, Ramp. Christ.' Then he hung up. Is that good?"

"Not looking good for a reference."

"I suppose not," Damon said. "So, what adventures await us today, sister?"

"Oh boy."

"Shopping?"

"Till we be dropping. Then we'll play private eye for a while. Should we get an office?"

"A private eye office?"

"Sure," Maricella said. "Maybe something downtown. An old walk-up with a reception area. Venetian blinds, a big old desk with a bottle of whiskey in the bottom drawer. Get a secretary. A coatrack to hang up our trench coats and fedoras. Then we could talk in 1940s detective slang."

"Or we could be rich, modern detectives who office in an elegant suite at the Hotel San Pablo. With room service and nice poofy towels and robes."

"You adapted quickly to the finer creature comforts of domestication."

"Quick study," Damon said.

"Let's go buy a car."

"Donating your Audi to the city impound lot?"

"For the time being," Maricella said. "It's a little too hot right now. And we need wheels. Should probably downgrade from my Audi, something a little less conspicuous. Any ideas?"

"Seventy-nine Lincoln Town Car do anything for you? In a lovely inconspicuous gold."

"Something in this century, please. But inconspicuous would be the thing to keep in mind. Should probably stay in the used category."

"See a lot of Ford Taurus's on the road," Damon said. "Popular fleet cars."

And a nice selection to choose from. There were five on the lot, an '03, an '05, and three '06s, two of which were light green. Maricella chose the light green one with five-spoke rims over the hubcapped one. At least it had a modicum of style, but not enough to undermine its undercover status. It had a cassette deck to boot, which puzzled both of them. Added to the puzzled list was the salesman, who was unaccustomed to someone buying a car with an American Express card. So much so that he had to check with his manager to see if he could put the deal through. But money's money, and the avoided hassle of filling out the requisite paperwork for financing a cool bonus.

Next came the clothes. Easy-breezy one-stop shopping at Macy's. The pure unadulterated pleasure of shopping without even a glance at a price. Like it, buy it, swipe the Amex, done. Maricella had bought a week's worth of wardrobe inside half an hour. And once Maricella was done she went to work on Damon. Which, once his sizes were determined, went just as quickly. Three blazers, three pairs of slacks, five shirts, two pairs of shoes, brown and black. Socks, belts, ties, time for lunch. Twenty grand before noon. The American Express card was made for people like Maricella. No limits.

Lunch was back at the hotel, where eager bellhops magically appeared to help with all the packages. Word had gotten around about Maricella, with hotel staff on special alert to attend to her every need. There was a bit of a letdown at the sight of the Taurus, it being so beneath her. Almost a sigh. But a twenty dollar bill to each of them gave them hope enough to carry on.

Before their Cobb salads and iced teas arrived for lunch, more phone calls were to be made. Maricella excused herself to take care of some affairs with regard to her father's funeral. Damon still couldn't think of him as his father, just as a weak old man with one hell of a life left behind. Damon's pondering about his real father's life was interrupted by the waiter.

"Phone call, Mr. Ramp." He handed Damon the phone.

"Hello?"

"Peek-a-boo, I see you."

Damon looked out the window. Hadji gave him a Michael Jackson move, with a crotch-grab finish. Then the heavy metal horns, with a slithering-tongue finish.

"You're mixing genres again," Damon said.

"Go with the flow, Jeth-ro. Where's the dish?"

"Phone call. Are you coming in or are you going to entertain me some more?"

"How 'bout both?"

"More show and tell?"

"You bet your hillbilly ass."

Forty Five

The Cobb salads and Hadji arrived at the same time. The look on his face suggested that it may have been his first encounter with a salad.

"Don't they have burgers here?" Hadji said.

"It is possible for lunches to exist without buns. And yes, they have wonderful burgers here. Want one?"

"Nah, I'm good."

"Do you eat?" Damon said. "Come to think of it, do you sleep? Go to school? Where have you been staying?"

"Do I have to answer all four, dad?" Hadji said. "Been to the Arches already and I don't get along with school. And it's a big world with lots of places to crash. Got two with that last one, notice?"

"And what else have you noticed?"

"Oh em fucking gee," Hadji said. "Gotta picture worth at least a couple thousand words. Shit's cray, man. Wanna see?"

Hadji pulled out his laptop and called up the aforementioned. He turned the screen toward Damon.

"Whaddaya spose in those long crates?" Hadji asked.

The room was stacked with boxes of roughly the same size, with long wooden crates along the back wall. Damon had seen similar crates before. All circuits on. An inventory search of his PC file suggested many possibilities in terms of what contents would require similar packaging. The search was refined by inputting all relevant detail germane to their current situation, which ruled out farm implements and the leg lamp from *A Christmas Story*.

"Weapons," Damon said. "Long guns, artillery, RPGs. Unmarked, black market military."

Maricella came back to the table. Damon turned the screen toward her.

"Storeroom at Petal," Damon said. "First guess, right off the top of your head."

"Drugs and guns. Usual suspects. Just like bacon and eggs," she said. "But the crates strike me as military, not something a typical street guy would use. But a business transaction is not out of the question. Someone's going to war."

"The big question is, *What is Rumples waiting for?*" Damon said. "He's gotta know what's going on here."

"Not necessarily all of it," Maricella said. "It's entirely possible that we know more than he does. And there are protocols for him to follow. Federal agents can't afford to guess the way we are. They need to know and be sure before they can move. Another thing, we're not even sure what they're after. We don't exactly have the whole picture either. And the follow-up to your big question is, *When do we tell him what we know?*"

"This is beyond serious to the nth degree," Damon said. "Rumples needs to know this. But we'll be sequestered if we tell him any of this. He'll want us off the playing field. He could lock us away for months. Anyone up for that?"

Both shook no.

"And we'd make lousy anonymous tipsters," Damon said. "We'd be whisked off to a federal safe house just as quickly."

"So we need someone to do the bidding for us," Maricella said.

"A pigeon," Damon said.

"Yes, a pigeon."

They both looked at Hadji.

"You're lousy role models," Hadji said.

"Indubitably," Damon said.

Forty Six

"Funeral's on Friday," Maricella said.

"Where?" Damon asked.

"It's here."

"St. Paul?"

"It gets even cozier. The reception after the funeral is right here at the hotel. The Saintly City is about to become Mob Central."

"My God, you actually said the word," Damon said.

"Ruh roh."

Damon was about to ask why everything was being held in St. Paul, but the words turned back on the way to his mouth. It was Times Square on New Year's Eve all over again, but this time the lights were playing a game of connect the dots. Disparate fragments of distant memories of his childhood—of his stepfather and pictures and places and feelings—were beginning to coalesce with new information and refined insight. A bridge that spanned his childhood to the present was being traversed. *Why St. Paul* was starting to make sense.

"Did our father actually live in St. Paul for a spell?" Damon asked.

"In the early days, when things got too hot in New York, he would cool off in St. Paul. I know sometimes he stayed in a house by the old St. Ambrose Church, up on Burr Street, an old Italian neighborhood on the lower East Side. And of course he did business here, so yeah, there's a definite history here. I'm kind of sketchy on the early days' stuff, but St. Paul has a rich history of underworld involvement. In fact, some of it is right across the street."

"Landmark Center. The old Federal Courts Building—FBI's old St. Paul field office, too."

"St. Paul's about to reconnect with its gangster past," Maricella said. "They all came through here—from Capone to Dillinger to Bugsy Siegel, Murder, Incorporated crews, cops, and politicians bought and paid for—St. Paul was a haven. They used to run bootleg right out of this hotel."

"Is the service at the Church of Saint Philippe, King of France?"

"Ah, yeah—mind telling me how you nailed that one?"

"I've been there before," Damon said. "A long time ago."

"You're remembering something."

"I was there with my stepfather. I couldn't have been more than five years old. And we weren't there to go to church. My stepfather was meeting someone. We were the only ones in the church, sitting in the first pew, by the altar. Then a man came in, wearing a long dark coat and hat, and my stepfather went to meet him. They spoke for a few minutes, then the man gave him a small package or envelope, and he was gone. My instincts are telling me that this was connected to our father—this was about me."

"Antonio and I are puzzled about the church," Maricella said. "All I know is that it's a little French church downtown. I don't know our father's or family's history there, this one's dropped right out of the clear blue. This came straight from his *consigliere*."

"Well, we're about five minutes away, maybe ten. We'll have to navigate around the Central Corridor light-rail line. In fact, I think the church is right on the line, on Cedar."

"Eliminates drive-by traffic in front of the church," Maricella said. "Interesting."

"Factored into the decision to have it there, perhaps?"

"Security is always near the top of the factor list, but there's a history there, too—and I want to know that history."

"No time like the present."

Forty Seven

Maricella turned onto East Tenth Street and did a slow U-turn where it dead-ended at the light-rail line, parking facing east. Damon was fascinated with how Maricella did things, and he just witnessed two extremely subtle but insightful glances into how she operated. The slow U-turn was slower than it had to be, as Tenth Street had a generous girth, due mainly to the fact that it was the home of St. Paul Fire Station 8, which was a ladder company. It was a *check if the coast is clear* look, and Damon watched her eyes dart off in at least a half dozen directions in a matter of seconds as she made the turn. Lay of the land. And parking so you're as close as possible to your destination was how everyone else did things, but not Maricella. Because it's all about the getaway. She parked not only facing east, but at the front of the line so she would have a clear shot in case she had to jam. And Damon conducted an experiment. As they exited the car he purposely buzzed the electronic door locks to lock up the car. Maricella, without a word, deactivated them. No time to fumble with a key or a fob to open up the car if you needed to move. Little things. Subtle things. But very important things. A lifetime of trained awareness. Done as naturally as putting on a sock.

"Well, not exactly the Cathedral, is it?" Maricella said as she darted off another series of glances around the area. "Spook over on Exchange."

Damon caught a glimpse of something dark moving out of the way across the street, on the Exchange Street side of the old McNally Smith College of Music building. Not quite a shadow, but a movement of light and energy. But Maricella saw it a split second faster.

"Gonna be a lot of eyeballs on this place this week," she said.

"Same guy, though."

"What same guy?"

"Emmanuel L. Masqueray," Damon said. "The same guy who designed this place designed the Cathedral, too. And the Basilica of Saint Mary in Minneapolis. But his favorite was this little French church. He called it his 'little gem.'"

"And you're my little weirdo," Maricella said. "Got any more geek to get out of your system before we continue?"

"Well, Masqueray was a student of the *École des Beaux-Arts* tradition. Came to St. Paul in 1905. The three bells in the towers are tuned to A, C, and E. Okay, I'm done now. Shall we?"

Damon gestured toward the old oak doors, weathered a parched blond by a hundred years of western exposure. They went inside.

"Oh my," Maricella said. "The stained glass is magnificent. What a beautiful little church."

"I remember sitting over there." Damon pointed toward the first pew, left of the altar. "My stepfather met the man in the dark coat just left of the front doors, in the shadows by the parish office. Come on, wait till you see the pipes of the organ—I remember thinking *this is what heaven looks like*, when I looked up at the pipes."

Maricella and Damon walked slowly down the aisle toward the altar. She was on his left, and each was looking off in their respective directions, taking in the rich ornamental details of the church. The density of the Beaux Arts grandeur was almost overwhelming to the eye, and Maricella slowed their pace to try and take it all in. Damon turned her around to look at the Casavant five division organ.

"I can see why this place made such a strong impression on you," Maricella said. "I've been to museums all over the world, but this is one of the most beautiful places I've ever seen. This organ alone is worth the price of admission. If they were going for heavenly, they sure hit the mark."

There were more flashes of movement in the side entryways, on both sides of the altar.

"We have more company," Damon said.

"We certainly do."

Damon sensed a relaxation in Maricella, a change so subtle that it was more feeling than something physical. A release of tension. Her shoulders and neck became more pliant, no longer contracted at full attention. She sidled closer to Damon, looking heavenward, soaking in the beauty, as if she was suddenly allowed to give herself freely to the art. She was safe and secure.

"Antonio is here."

Forty Eight

The flashes of movement in the side entryways were Antonio's personal security detail. Why Maricella relaxed. She recognized one without showing a hint of recognition to Damon. Controlling body movement. No knee-jerk reactions, controlling something as fundamental as damping the natural inclination to look at someone you know. Skills that cannot be taught. A nurtured family trait that Damon missed out on, but was trained to recognize. Different skill sets. But allied in concert, a formidable force.

Antonio appeared in the entryway on the left side of the altar—the Tenth Street side, which made perfect sense. Security made sure the coast was clear, light-rail tracks to the west, fire station to the north, out of the car, across the sidewalk and into the building. Antonio showed no surprise at seeing Maricella, or that she was with Damon. But his gaze was trained at Maricella. He motioned her over.

Antonio's gaze continued in the general direction of Maricella, watching her move down the aisle to meet him. But he glanced at Damon briefly, a look that not only was an acknowledgment of his presence, but had the addendum of a slight nod, that Damon interpreted as a nod of approval. The look told Damon that he was simply pleased that both of them were safe, after the tumult up north.

Maricella and Antonio conferred briefly, as though they were associates discussing a business matter rather than a brother and sister sorting through the difficulties of a father's funeral. There were no hugs or excitations, save for a congenial touch of Maricella's elbow from Antonio as he was making a point. There was an obvious familial connection between the two, but it was a guarded and distant closeness. Maybe it had to be that way, by virtue of the lives they led. And then he was gone.

"Did Antonio shed any light on our father's history here at the church?" Damon asked.

"Only that this was his wish. That this wasn't a family decision or a decision based on security or anything else. Our father specified *this* place—and it's driving me crazy. Something happened here, something significant or symbolic. I don't know...is this some kind of atonement or penance? Our father wasn't exactly a regular parishioner here. And yes, I think you're somehow connected to all of this."

"Anyone left to ask who might have been around at the time?"

"I can only think of one," Maricella said. "It's our Uncle Rigo— our father's younger brother—and he'll be here on Friday. Everyone else is gone."

"Rigo?"

"Short for Amerigo—as in Vespucci. You know."

"I do. Uncle Rigo. Nice. How much younger?"

"He's eighty-nine," Maricella said.

"Marbles still intact?"

"Not counting on total recall, but he's all we've got."

Damon spotted a young priest coming from the side entrance to the right of the altar. He stopped to genuflect before turning up the aisle toward Damon and Maricella. He smiled warmly as their eyes met.

"Not necessarily," Damon said.

"Good afternoon," the priest said. "I'm Father Guerrier. May I be of any assistance to you?"

"Yes, as a matter of fact, you could be of great assistance to my sister and I," Damon said. "Do you have a record of the priests who served here, and the years of their tenures?"

"All the way back to the founding in 1868," Father Guerrier said. "Of course I would need permission from the Pastor to give you that information. May I inquire as to why you are asking for this information?"

"Go ahead, sister, you take this one."

"You see, our father recently passed, and his service is here, this Friday," Maricella began. "But we're truly puzzled as to why our father insisted that his service be here. We have no family history here that we know of, he wasn't a regular parishioner here, yet there's got to be some kind of connection to this place. We were thinking that maybe the priest here back in the sixties might shed a little light on our situation, because we think the history stems from around that period."

"My deepest condolences on the loss of your father," Guerrier said. "We are talking about Giuseppe Naimo, are we not?"

"We are," Maricella said.

"Then you may add my name to the list of the puzzled, because I have torn through our archives here from stem to stern, and there isn't a hint of a trace of your father. And I mean absolutely nothing— which is highly unusual."

"May I inquire as to why *you* were searching for this information?" Damon asked.

"Mea culpa. *The devil made me do it*," Guerrier said with lusty whisper. Then he straightened. "Truthfully, I am the theologian in residence here, and I spend a great deal of time here studying every aspect of this church. And, combined with my great interest and passion for history and paleography—and perhaps some interest of the everyday scintillating variety—I, honestly, simply was curious."

"Seen a lot of strange faces today?" Maricella asked.

"Since early this morning. Our little French church is suddenly very popular."

"We need to talk to the Pastor?"

It was the way she broke the ice. The way it was said. There were words omitted in her query that she conveyed in the cadence of her question. There was a look too. Translation: *Do we really need to talk to the Pastor?* No way he could resist. He was too curious. He was going to look it up as soon as they left anyway.

"Well, I really shouldn't..."

Bingo.

Forty Nine

Damon was picturing an ancient alcove deep within the bowels of the church, its shelves filled with illuminated manuscripts and ornate handwritten parish ledgers, written in a flowing cursive, each letter a work of art in and of itself. Time-honored craftsmanship, undertaken with great fastidious care. Penmanship of a baroque age, now the sole province of the calligraphy set.

He settled for a five-year-old Dell in a nondescript upstairs office.

Father Guerrier opened a file of names and dates, written in twelve-point Times New Roman. Clean and efficient, fastidiousness of a different age. He scrolled down to the era Maricella had expressed interest in.

"Father Marcel Claremboux, 1962 to 1971," Guerrier said.

Maricella looked at Damon and shrugged.

Father Guerrier typed in his name and clicked. Scrolled and clicked.

"Deceased 1973," he said.

"Were there others?" Damon asked. "He had to have an assistant, right?"

"Not listed here."

Father Guerrier got up and went to a pair of gray metal filing cabinets. Flipped through a row of files and pulled out a manila folder. Slid out a yellowed, typewritten sheet.

"Here it is," he said. "Father Paulo Monreale, 1962 to 1964."

"Is that French?" Damon asked.

"Monreale is in Sicily," Maricella said. "Right next to Corleone. Our maternal grandmother was from Monreale."

Father Guerrier perked up like a kid who just heard the bells of the ice cream truck.

"Seriously?" Damon said.

"Uh-huh."

"Oh, wait—deceased 1964," Guerrier said.

"Cause of death?" Damon asked.

"Not here."

"Natural causes," a voice said from the doorway, turning everyone around. "If you believe it natural for a thirty-one-year-old man in perfect health to suddenly just up and die."

Rumples. Leaning against the door jamb, arms loosely crossed. He scratched his chin to coax some more words out.

"Body was repatriated back to Sicily, too," he said. "Expedited manner. Highly unusual for such a modest young priest to be so highly connected, but I digress. Hello, Miss Naimo, so nice to see you again. And Mr. Ramp—mighty wrestler of mean branches—healing up nicely, I see. Sorry to so rudely interrupt, Father. Special Agent William Charles, FBI. Lovely little church you have here."

"So what's the special of the day, Agent Charles?" Maricella said.

Rumples wasted no time seizing his opportunity. It was time to play a little poker, a game he was very good at it. He was holding something, something substantial, but nobody knew exactly what. But he knew more than Maricella or Damon or the young priest. Pure bluffs never happen. You have to have something to start with.

He opened strong. Maricella locked down ice-cold.

"Oh, a very special offer for you, Miss Naimo," Rumples said. "I bringeth answers to all that you desire. A simple exchange of information is all I ask."

"You want me to roll on my brother," Maricella said, with a savvy toughness that rivaled the hardest of wiseguys.

Father Guerrier clasped his hands behind his head and leaned back in his chair, his mouth slightly agape with wonder and delight. All he needed was some popcorn.

"Right to the point as always, Miss Naimo," Rumples said. "You never disappoint. Daddy would be very proud of you. And you want to know all about Daddy and this church, don't you?"

"Why, that sounded like a downright taunt, Agent Charles," Maricella said. "Go bleep yourself. Sorry, Father."

"Forgiven," Guerrier said. "That wasn't very nice."

"If you're gonna take sides, Father, take the side of someone whose family hasn't broken every single one of the Ten Commandments ten times over," Rumples said. "A simple quid pro quo is all I'm asking, Miss Naimo. It's done every day. No big whoop."

"Pretty big whoop where I come from, Charles," Maricella said. "In fact, they don't come much bigger. No dice."

Maricella was good at poker, too. She showed no signs of weakness, even though it was driving her crazy inside. Rumples *knew*. She knew it. Damon knew it.

"Look, I'm trying to stop a war here, Miss Naimo," Rumples said. "There's some pretty big hitters in town, and a whole lotta shit is about to hit the fan."

"And you know what to do when that's about to happen, don't you, Agent Charles?" Maricella said.

"Oh joy. Back to the cheeky," Rumples said. "Uh...duck?"

"Unplug the fan."

Fifty

"You have what military personnel call the 'thousand-yard stare,'" Damon said to Maricella. "Maybe working through the particulars will help."

"I know just the place," she said.

The place was the Tophat Bar, a blue-collar joint on the eastern fringe of downtown. The Tophat's clientele was a mixed bag of bums, hipsters, and white-collars, who threaded their way around the bums to order the bar's famous coneys. Damon and Maricella were sitting at the bar inside of ten minutes, from church to barstool.

"Two coneys and a Bud," Maricella said.

"Same," Damon said.

There was one other guy in the bar, six stools down, who looked like a regular. Whiskey or brandy water in front of him, five days' worth of salt-and-pepper stubble on his face, matted, greasy brownish hair and clothes, probably missing some teeth. Damon already knew what he would smell like. And that he would be down for a visit before he and Maricella headed for the door. An immutable law of the universe.

"So, the game is still afoot with Rumples," Damon began. "You know you could have a bargaining chip in knowing about the weapons and drug cache at Petal, if you played it right. Probably get Rumples to deal about what he knows about our father and the church—all without you rolling on our brother, or putting us in protective custody. I think I know why you're standing pat, but I want to hear what you're thinking."

"One, the chip isn't mine to bargain with. It's off the table, and my gut is telling me to keep it that way. That's what we all agreed on, and I still think it's the best way to go. Agreed?"

"Agreed."

"Two, we know Charles knows more than we do about our father and the church. That's the hand he's betting with, but there might be some bluffing in there as well. It's very possible that he got dead-ended before he could find out the whole story of our father and the church. He's a shrewd player and he just may be throwing out some bait to see if I bite."

Damon smiled. He could see Rumples in the old fishing hat again.

"Fishing."

"Yep, fishing," Maricella said. "It's the way he's played for as long as I've known him. It's always been that way between the FBI and all the families. Fish, catch a few, then you negotiate; you give us this, we'll give you that. Making deals is how they do business. It's the best of the best going at it, and both sides are so compartmentalized. The damage is always so controlled. A few bite the dust, but both parties always come out alive and live to fight another day."

"But the look was telling me that it's driving you crazy not knowing about all of this. And the waiting is going to make you even more crazy."

"Controlling the craziness is what it's all about. Unkept emotions do people in every day. It's law enforcement's best friend. Think Dostoyevsky's *Crime and Punishment*. Some people just can't carry the load. They burst."

"Like the breakdowns on the stand of almost every episode of *Perry Mason*," Damon said. "I used to tune in just at the end of the show for the dramatics. It's very entertaining."

"*Perry Mason* was the greatest show...Hamitten Burger...Lieutenant Raggs...Della Boulevard or Street or whatfuckin'ever. Goddam fuckin' lawyers...*whoosh*—you work around here, honey?"

The man at the bar had stealthily made his way down to Damon and Maricella. Waited for his moment. He smelled bad but his timing was good. Broca's area a little messed up, but no inhibitions to speak of, so it was pretty much a wash.

Coneys were up.

"They have the greatest coneys..." Whiskey started in again.

"Yes, they do. We're going to eat now, okay?" Maricella said, clearly and patiently.

"Okay, honey," Whiskey said. "That your boyfriend? What happened to his face?"

The general rule around the Tophat was that you were on your own. No staff was going to intervene on your behalf. You were responsible for your own bum control. They held true to libertarian principles at the Tophat, warts, bums, and all.

Whiskey made his way back down to his camp one barstool at a time. He was walking with his hands as much as his feet, his hands pushing off the stools to keep himself upright, his legs coming along for the ride. He wanted to go out for a smoke—smoking anywhere inside now being verboten—but he needed to rest first. "Goddam government..."

The coneys were good right off the line, no doctoring with ketchup or mustard necessary. They were served on buttery grilled buns, greasy done right. And a fresh pair of ice-cold beers to wash them down.

"Okay, point-blank, right off the top of your head," Damon said. "What's your gut tell you on Rumples? Does he know the whole story or not?"

"He knows," Maricella said. "But his prices are way too high. I'm not rolling on anybody, let alone my brother or our family. So we try our other option and wait."

"Uncle Rigo."

"He's a sweet, little old Italian man," Maricella said. "Kind of short and roly-poly from too many raviolis."

"I'll look for more options."

"Do."

Fifty One

Whiskey had made his way outside for a smoke while Damon and Maricella finished their coneys. The notorious three o'clock wall must have come suddenly, as he seemed well into his late afternoon siesta, although his choice of location left something to be desired. Walmart had nothing on the Tophat Bar, which had upped the ante by employing the first horizontal people greeter. Whiskey could now add *human speed bump* to his illustrious resumé.

Damon and Maricella sidestepped Whiskey to make their way to her car. But they stopped to watch a fast-moving parade of silenced police cars, which were coming from all directions, in all their incarnations. Some marked, some un, standard prowl cars to SUVs to speedy interceptors. Strobes on, sirens off. Silent urgency. Something big.

All converging on the general area around the Church of St. Philippe, King of France.

Damon's PC file didn't have to break a sweat on this one. He turned to Maricella.

"That's no coincidence."

Maricella was looking down at Whiskey. Something was telling her that the situation wasn't right. She prodded him with her foot.

Damon picked up on it too. Whiskey was sprawled on his stomach. He wasn't moving. Maricella lifted up his shoulder to have a look at his front side. She revealed a pool of blood around his throat.

"He's been shot."

Damon and Maricella both looked up, both eyeballing a rough trajectory of where the shot came from.

"Also no coincidence," Damon said.

"No shit, Sherlock."

"With the guff again, sister," he said.

"He—"

They both started at the same time.

"He—"

"God, we must be related," Maricella said. "You were saying, Mr. Holmes?"

"Think he saw something he shouldn't have?" Damon said.

"Either that or it was a little target practice," Maricella said. "The latter being highly unlikely."

The heavenly warmth of neurotransmission was accompanied by a film, special to the occasion. Damon narrated the short film to Maricella.

"He was standing here having a smoke, looking up at the skyline," Damon explained. "The shooter was up high enough to have a view of the church as well as the bar. He was calibrating his scope, using multiple landmarks. The bum spotted him, but that wasn't enough to make the shooter fire. He pointed at him, as if to say *I see you*—probably thought Big Brother was watching. The shooter knew he was spotted. He had to take the bum out."

"Risky, but plausible," Maricella said. "A mechanic with a muzzle suppressor. Not a sound except the fleshy thump of impact and the body hitting the ground. And daylight, so no muzzle flash. After three on a Monday, not a lot of eyeballs. Plausible."

"Bartender calling this one in?" Damon said.

"Probably best," Maricella said. "I don't want to be answering questions for the next three days."

She went inside to inform the bartender that one of his customers was taking a nap outside his door. Nothing to be all rushed about. He nodded in acknowledgment and went about putting the rest of a case of beer in the cooler.

Maricella rejoined Damon out on the sidewalk.

"Well, where to, sister?"

"Think I forgot something at the church," she said.

"Thought so."

Fifty Two

The hubbub was west of the church, nearly two blocks west on Exchange Street. The cluster of police officers and paramedics suggested that they were surrounding a body on the street. They obviously hadn't connected the body to the goings-on at the church, as Damon and Maricella were standing right in front of it, and they were paying it no mind. Their sheer numbers indicated that they responded to a shooting, so somebody heard something, or must have discovered the gunshot victim or seen the body go down.

The FBI contingent had a deeper insight as to the current goings-on, and joined Damon and Maricella on the steps of the church. He elected to kick-off rather than receive.

"And to think it's only Monday," Rumples said. "I'm feeling a pretty busy week coming on. You?"

"Aren't you going to crash the party?" Maricella said. "Offer a little insight. You know, spirit of cooperation and all that."

"Not really up for all that right now," Rumples said. "Besides, I got a guy over there. Waiting for an ID."

"Think he's carrying a driver's license on him?" Maricella said. She smirked at Rumples. A knowing, snarky smirk to boot.

"Know something I don't, Miss Naimo?"

"Got a bonus something, too," she said. Smirk plus eyebrow raise.

"Should we volley it around a few more times, just for sport?" Rumples said. "Job satisfaction's pretty good on your end, isn't it?"

"'Tis."

"Like in on this, Mr. Ramp?"

"I really enjoyed that," Damon said.

Maricella nodded toward the crime scene. "He's probably the advance guy we saw earlier, skulking around the church. And there's another guy down in front of the Tophat Bar—just some bum who probably saw something he shouldn't have."

"Well, saints be praised—cooperation," Rumples said.

Then the gravity of what he was just told did what gravity does, bringing him closer to earth. He sat down on the steps and pushed his hair back with both hands. Pulled out his cell and relayed the information he was just given. Got some in return.

"Nine millimeter," he said, to no one in particular.

The thousand-yard stare had transferred to Agent Charles. Then his phone buzzed. He listened and looked, puffed out an agitated sigh. The effects of the gravity wore off. He was up on his feet.

"Looks like everyone hit the ground running this week," Rumples said. "Three bodies down three different ways. Jesus, Joseph and Mary."

He shoved the phone toward Maricella.

"Know dis guy?" he said, his Chicago accent thick and gnarled, a tinge of exasperation.

Damon felt Maricella shudder, but she didn't show it in her face. Rumples didn't pick up on it. Damon craned his head to get around the glare for a better look. It stood up the hair on his arms and neck.

"Can't say I do," Maricella said. "Doesn't look like I'll get a chance to either."

"An absolute ice-cold martini," Rumples said. "Yeah, yeah, Grey Goose…" he grumbled as he walked away.

"That wasn't who I thought it was, was it?" Damon said. "God, I can't even say—"

"Not to mention your grammar," Maricella said. "Did you see the look on his face, with his eyes and mouth open like that?"

"A look of terror or surprise," Damon said. "Like he was horrified or in excruciating pain."

"It even shook Charles up," Maricella said. She shuddered again. "It's doing a number on me, too."

"Because you know what this ultimately means."

"That the guy who just took out one of the most lethal men in the world has some unfinished business," Maricella said.

"Such as clipping the strings of the guy who just sicced *Diavolo Nero* on him."

"Antonio."

"Pashtun's starting to take care of things personally."

"He already took one run at Antonio up north, but he wasn't on the trigger," Maricella said. "Now it's going to come down really hard. He's about as nasty as it gets."

"Noticing you're not saying the name," Damon said.

"Martini might help."

"I know just the place."

Fifty Three

True to her word, Maricella did prefer Grey Goose martinis. Served up, double olive, the second one accompanied by a jumbo shrimp cocktail. Served with a smile, but with distracted, darting eyes. Nervous eyes.

Not the usual Monday night crowd at the San Grille.

Lucky for Damon, Maricella was an excellent tour guide.

"Remember *Romper Room?*" she asked, midway through martini number two. Timing was about right. "You know, I see *Jimmy* and *Jenny* and *Billy...*"

"A little before my time," Damon said. "But if they did it today, it would be more like, I see *Jaimarquis* and *Jennikesha* and *Billamountaingrass...* But I digress. The floor's all yours, sister."

"You'll be doing stand-up soon," Maricella said. "Well, I see Knuckles, and Joey Bongos, and Diamond Fats, and Two Stools—the latter two being pretty self-explanatory due to their stout nature. And there's about a half mil in suits and Rolexes in the other room. Barkeep looks nervous now, but he'll be smiling at the end of the night when he counts his tips. These guys really know how to swing."

"Are pinky rings and tinted glasses requirements of the uniform?"

"It's in the manual."

"Anyone from the other team?"

"Feds? Like remoras on a shark. When Guido comes to town it's all hands on deck. Trust me, there are eyes and ears—electronic and otherwise—everywhere."

"Mob Central."

"This is about as close as it gets to a convention."

The bartender with the darting eyes walked over with phone in hand. "Excuse me, are you Damon Ramp?"

"I am."

He blew out a sigh of relief. "Good. Really didn't want to visit table three. Those guys are really giving me the look. Oh, phone call." He handed Damon the phone.

"Hello?"

No answer.

"I think they want refills," Maricella said to the bartender. "What are they drinking?"

"Macallan eighteen-year-old—it's thirty-eight bucks a throw."

"Hello?"

Still no answer.

"I got it," Maricella said. "Give me the bottle."

Maricella moseyed over to table three.

"Gentlemen," she started. "Allow me." She topped off their glasses.

"Hey, Mare, how you doin'?" Joey Bongos said. "Hey, sorry about your pop, kid."

"Yeah, all respects, Mary," Diamond Fats said.

They all bowed their heads.

"*Salúte, Don Naimo,*" they all said, raising their glasses.

"Hey," Knuckles whispered, motioning Maricella closer with a couple flicks of his finger. "Who's the nebbish?" He nodded toward Damon.

"Him you'll want to meet," Maricella said. "Damon?"

Damon gave up on the phone call and walked over to table three, which gave him the once-over through tinted glass. Table three began to snicker.

"You really gotta watch yourself around those cats," Two Stools said, his jowls and chins quivering like Jell-O.

"That's some mean fucking pussy," Diamond Fats added, throwing his three hundred quivering pounds into the mix.

They all knocked their pinky rings on the table, accompanied by some gold bracelet jangle.

Maricella turned her back to the table and faced Damon. She removed his glasses and pushed his hair back and off to the side. Then she introduced him.

"Gentlemen, Damonico Naimo."

Table three fell silent. But the jowls and chins were still quivering. Something about momentum and some guy named Newton. Scotch, too.

"Sorry. Can't get past the cat thing," Knuckles said.

A thousand pounds of Guido in Armani and a hundred grand in gold and watches were shaking table three down to its foundation. They stopped laughing long enough to knock back another hundred and fifty bucks of Scotch. Maricella topped off their glasses again.

"We really gotta do something about those scratches," she said to Damon.

"No shit, Sherlock."

"Did you just mock me?"

"Guff and sass are probably right around the corner," Damon said.

"Is there an open-mic night somewhere I can take you to? Suddenly you're a comedian. Know any good jokes?"

"Hey, I got one," Joey Bongos said. "A priest and a bobcat walk into a bar..."

"Well, that ship just sailed," Maricella said to Damon. "No turning back once the jokes start."

"Phone call, Mr. Ramp," the bartender called out.

"Hello?"

"'Bout time you chimed in, Jethro. Havin' fun with all the Guidos?"

"It's like I went back in a time machine and stumbled onto the set of *Goodfellas*," Damon said. "Where are you?"

"What, am I past curfew, dad? I'm around close enough to see the Guido convention. I've never seen so many suits and pinky rings in all my life. What, is there like some special mob store where they get all this shit?"

Damon could see it perfectly. Glass display cases filled with pinky rings and gold bracelets and tinted glasses. A spinning rack of religious necklaces to guide and comfort any Guido adversity or anxiety. Racks of shiny suits. Gun holsters for every occasion. Short guy with a mustache in a white shirt with a loosened tie and suspenders, tape measure draped around his neck. At the beck and call of every wiseguy need.

"Has our pigeon flown the coop yet?" Damon asked.

"Up, up and away," Hadji said.

"How?"

"USB flash with a nice little slide presentation of the back rooms of our favorite flower shop. Threw in a picture of Kate Upton for giggles. Freakin' A—there is a god."

"This is all just a walk in the park for you, isn't it?" Damon said.

"It's a beautiful day in the neighborhood, homes."

Fifty Four

The wake-up call came in at a minute past five. Damon didn't recall asking for one, but he also had never consumed martinis before. Not to mention the beer. The hypochondriacal area of his brain wondered if he needed to call AA. What if Whiskey had infected him with some kind of bizarre bum parasite? Was that the coneys backing up or a myocardial infarction? But his most immediate need was to stop all that annoying ringing.

"Hello?"

"Rise and shine, Jethro. Turn on Channel Three."

Damon tried to turn the TV on with the phone. He woke up a little more, then grabbed the remote. He fumbled through some buttons before finding Channel Three. The closed captioning ended up in Cyrillic. The image was a crime scene, red and blue strobes flashing everywhere. It was really windy. The young female reporter in the trench coat was not going to like what her hair looked like on TV.

"What am I looking at?" Damon asked.

"Pre-dawn raid at Petal," Hadji said. "Don't know if Johnny Law scored or not. Betty Reporter can't get anyone to talk to her. She's just chasing her cute little tail around, describing a 'large scale law enforcement raid.' But she knows more than she can tell right now."

Hadji's last sentence woke Damon up fully and got his systems up and running. Data began to stream. PC file kicked in first.

"Oh, Hadji—did it have to be an anchorpigeon?" Damon said. "What kind of deal did you strike?"

"Pretty damn good one," Hadji said. "Heh-heh, yummy fresh anchorpigeon. Good one, homes."

"What am I going to do with you? You gotta...I don't know—stop extorting people!"

"Oh, don't get yourself all up in a bind, Jethro. I didn't get too greedy. It was just one of those two birds with one stone deals. Got a creeper to stop creepin', got us a pigeon to deliver, and made a few bucks to boot. Heh-heh—actually a threefer. Fourfer if you count Ron Burgundy cashing in on the scoop. Nothin' but winners showing up on my scorecard."

"What's going on?" Maricella said, tousling her hair and stifling a yawn as she entered the room.

Damon pointed at the TV.

"Did the commies take over our TV?"

"Hey, is that the dish?" Hadji said. "Lemme say how-do, Jethro."

Damon handed her the phone. "He'll explain."

"Hello?"

"Buy you a cup of coffee, doll? Whatcha wearing?"

"Oh, for Christ's sake—don't you sleep? Or ever stop being you? Is there an off switch somewhere?"

"You can frisk me anytime, doll."

"Ahhrgh!" Maricella dropped the phone and looked at Damon. "Just explain it to me later. I'm going to take a shower now and try to wash off everything that just happened to me."

Damon retrieved the phone.

"Heh-heh."

"What else do you have planned for the day?" Damon said.

"I'll be sure to think of something."

"No more extorting, okay?"

"C'mon, Jethro—guy's gotta eat."

"You've extorted enough to buy a chain of restaurants."

"Maybe I want to expand into other markets."

"God bless it—just take a day off, wouldja?"

"And do what, go to fuckin' Disneyland? Catfish a-jumpin', Jethro. Gonna check out this scene and see what's what. Like to start with a peek up Betty Reporter's trench coat. Heh-heh."

"You're on-scene?"

"Wanna see?"

"No!"

"You're no fun, Jethro. You need to get out more."

"How long have you been there?"

"I was on-scene before Betty was. Hell, I watched the Johnny Laws roll in. Pretty freakin' cool. Damn, those guys are sneaky fast. Whatcha drivin' at, homes?"

"They pull anything out of there yet?"

"Not that I can see. But I can't see around back, they got it all cordoned off."

"Any vehicles leave the scene?"

"Negative."

"There's no alley, so they'd have to take Grand. Wanna sneak around back and see what's what?"

"I'll kick it around back. But keep an eye on Betty, 'cause I'm gonna lose the frontal."

"Roger that."

Maricella was still toweling off her hair as she reentered the room. "Roger what?"

"That," Damon said, pointing at the TV. "Feds raided Petal."

Maricella tuned into the TV for a minute. Damon rested his eyes.

"Oh good heavens!" she said.

"What—what?" Damon said.

"Why is *he* on TV?" Maricella said. "And what...on God's green earth is he doing?"

"I think he's twerking."

"Oh my God."

"At least he's not extorting anyone."

Fifty Five

A click through the local channels confirmed that the other news stations now had reporters on-scene at the raid. The pictures being shown had import and conveyed a sense of something big happening, as only the flash of law enforcement lights can do. TV likes flashy, shiny things, and takes to them like a cat chasing around a laser pointer. Problem was, they had nothing to report. Which pretty much put them on par with the cat in the smarts department. If a cat figured out how to say "Good morning" it could do their job.

Perhaps due to her encounter with Hadji, Maricella was all fired up and felt like something spicy for breakfast. The Market Cafe at the hotel was happy to oblige, and the Andouille Benedict seemed to do the trick. Not wanting to exacerbate his paranoidal thoughts of myocardial infarction, Damon stuck with the blander, traditional Benedict. He ate at a leisurely pace, taking twice as long as Maricella to put away his breakfast, often taking a break between bites to peruse through one of the five newspapers Maricella bought at the gift shop. And he had plenty of time for chit-chat.

"Phone call, Mr. Ramp."

Maricella slid over a five dollar bill toward their server.

"Sorry about all the phone calls."

"He gets more calls than the president," the server said.

"I think he's trending," Maricella said.

"Just gotta watch himself around those cats."

"I'll pass that along."

"Hello?"

"Something ain't clicking, Jethro."

"Such as?"

"Big-ass FBI panel truck parked around back. Problem is, ain't nothing going in it. And they don't look happy. I think they got skunked."

"Still getting a feed from there?"

"Negative. They pulled my wires. Everything went black."

"Tipped off?"

"That'd be my guess. But man, that timeline's tight. Pretty damn good bleepin' tipping to hit that window."

"I'm seeing two possibilities," Damon said. "One is that the tipping came from inside the Bureau. Care to guess the second?"

"Fuck—anchorpigeon."

"Maybe trying to buy the other blackmailers off his back."

"But doesn't that screw his story? What about the scoop?"

"He got the scoop—they were the first ones there to get pictures. The bragging rights are already in the bag. Really doesn't matter if they find anything or not."

"Damn. Sorry, homes. My bad. Ooh...Eliot Ness gonna be wicked pissed."

"And...I am about to find out how pissed. In about thirty seconds."

Damon and Maricella watched Rumples steam through the lobby, his head on a swivel, eyes darting side to side. He creased his eyes and furrowed his brow when he spotted them.

"Very pissed," Damon said to Hadji, clicking off.

"That's one angry bear," Maricella said. "I'll buy him some breakfast, that might help."

Rumples slowed and tried to compose himself, now that his quarry had been spotted. He pulled up a chair and let his blood pressure come down a couple of ticks. He looked at the menu. He hummed. Whistled softly.

"Ah...good morning, Agent Charles," Maricella started. "Buy you some breakfast?"

"Yes you can," Rumples said. "Least you can do."

"Whatever do you mean, Agent Charles?" Maricella said. "Get up on the wrong side of the bed?"

"Right side and plenty early, which segues nicely to our next subject." He hummed some more, and ordered some steel cut oatmeal and orange juice.

"And here I thought you were going to try and break the bank," Maricella said. "I was willing to go full entrée. Or are you going for the extra fiber?"

"Ah, bank," he said. "Vaults...remember Geraldo Rivera?"

Maricella looked puzzled, but Damon knew where he was going.

"Al Capone's vaults," Damon said. "1986. Thirty million people tuned in for two hours for a couple of empty bottles."

"Made him look like an idiot," Rumples said.

"But millions of people finally learned the correct usage of *anticlimactic*," Damon said.

Rumples went to work on his oatmeal. "A complete idiot..." he mumbled between spoonfuls. He mumbled other things while he ate, but Damon and Maricella couldn't understand what he was saying. Then he got a phone call.

He said one word before clicking off and wiping his mouth.

"Okay."

Fifty Six

The term "okay" has several meanings and connotations depending on usage and context. It can mean approval or agreement, or simply mean all right or all correct, the latter being a derivation of the Dutch term *oll korrect*. Some trace its etymology to the Choctaw Indians, while others trace it back to Martin Van Buren's 1840 campaign, where he was referred to as "Old Kinderhook." It can be an adverb, adjective, verb, and sometimes a noun. It can be "OK" or "okay." But Damon had been around enough government and law enforcement types to know another meaning, in which the aforementioned term serves as a disguise for another word, when it is expedient to their needs. For instance, the context in which Rumples used the term, so as not to cause alarm to his guests.

Hence, his nonchalant "okay" meant something else entirely to whoever was on the other end of that line.

Go.

Suddenly a different brand of suit had taken over the lobby of the Hotel San Pablo. The sleek, stylish lines of Armani had been supplanted by the crisp, clean lines of Brooks Brothers. Pinky rings were out, earpieces attached to squiggly cords were in. These guys knew how to swing, too, but they learned their steps in Quantico, Virginia, as opposed to Brooklyn or the Bronx. But the direction of their steps was unmistakable. Maricella looked at Damon and said something uncharacteristically unladylike. Damon concurred, but did not swear. Only when he was hiking.

Rumples had had enough. Six federal agents in dark suits surrounded their table.

"Are we under arrest?" Maricella asked.

"If you resist you will be," Rumples said. He threw his cloth napkin on the table and walked away. One of the agents gestured with an open, guiding hand.

This way.

A black Suburban with tinted windows and a forest of antennas on its roof was waiting. So was the rest of the family.

"Road trip," Hadji said.

Maricella and Damon filed in next to him. Maricella tried to squirm out of her seating assignment, but got stuck next to Hadji.

"Hiya, doll." Hadji put his head on her shoulder.

"Remove it or you're going to the hospital," Maricella said.

"Jethro! Whaddaya know, homes?"

"Why are you so darn chipper?" Damon asked.

"Adventure!" Hadji exclaimed. "And I just slammed a Monster." He started bouncing in his seat. "C'mon, snappity, Jeeves, time to drive Miss Daisy to the sto'. Ah-oooo!"

"I should have resisted," Maricella said. "Jail would have been quicker." They sped off from the hotel. "Bye nice poofy towels and robes..."

"Thanks for letting me be rich for a couple of days, sister."

"You're welcome. Glad you enjoyed it."

"Where do you suppose we're going?"

"Not the Four Seasons," Maricella said.

"Driver, may I ask where we are going?" Damon asked.

"North," one of the agents said.

North it was, on I-35E out of the city inside of five minutes. Déjà vu for Damon, except Guido was downright loquacious compared to what he was getting out of the Brooks Brothers. Of course there was also the change of cars and the game show mask laced with a Mickey. Well, the north part was the same.

And the game show masks came out eventually, it just took longer than Damon's last adventure with Guido. Right after the rest stop in Hinckley, sans Mickey Finn sleep aid.

"Seriously?" Damon said.

"I'm afraid I'll have to insist, sir," one of the Brooks Brothers said.

At least he didn't threaten him with option two.

They put on the masks. These ones didn't share the complex, dense odor of the Guido model. And it didn't take Hadji long to go into his blind man bit, his wandering hands always seeming to land on Maricella.

While Maricella was batting away Hadji's wandering hands, Damon called up his GP file. He opened a map of the area, pinning their start point, and began surveying all the highway options along the way. He could determine compass directions by the list of the bulky Suburban, which was made more pronounced by the driver's haste to get to his assigned location. It was like following a blip on a virtual map. All he had to do was stay awake.

All he had to do...

Goodnight, Mr. Ramp.

Fifty Seven

The couch was warm but uncomfortably damp and smelled of wood smoke and a deep-set mustiness, as though it had been that way for a considerable time. Ditto for the afghan, though its garish array of mottled oranges and browns and blacks at least served as a signpost as to how long they had been that way, that had Damon guessing 1970s. And it was short. Damon was all bunched up in an elongated fetal position, and he had a crick in his neck thanks to a hard, lumpy throw pillow.

And it had a twin. Love seats.

Maricella was writhing in similar discomfort on the other side of a smoke and ring-stained coffee table, which hadn't seen a coaster since Sister Sledge was on the charts. Hadji was sprawled out on a bearskin rug in front of the fireplace, like he was their Labrador retriever. They were all coming around at the same time. They all had the same *what the hell* look on their faces. Maricella went first. First order of business, stay calm, be logical, establish location.

"Where the hell are we?" Maricella said. Good enough for starters. "Any ideas, Mr. Wizard?" she said to her brother.

"Starting with the sass, I see," Damon said. "Guff is sure to follow. One moment please."

Damon booted up his operating systems, then called up his GP file to try and establish location. Problem was, there wasn't enough inputting data. The best he could come up with was that it was still light out, and the last time *his* lights were on was in Hinckley. There were no clocks, no TV, no radio, no phone, and they had confiscated Damon's watch and Hadji's phone. They had been knocked out at least two hours, so they could have been anywhere inside a two-hour radius of Hinckley. For all Damon knew, they could have just turned around and headed back to the Cities. He narrowed it down to Minnesota or Wisconsin. He looked out the window. There was a faded red barn paired with a hundred-year-old silo and lots of prairie. And a dark Suburban parked sideways down the road. There were places like that fifteen minutes out of St. Paul, sans the government Suburban. It looked like a hobby farm. *Results inconclusive.* He went with the sass.

"Best guess? *Green Acres.*"

The room was generic and nondescript, with an equally imaginative single-story floor plan: living room, small kitchen, bathroom off said kitchen, and two bedrooms on the end. It had a stone fireplace that looked like an accident waiting to happen. The paintings that hung on the walls were products of the generic hobby farm school movement, whose still lifes were fixed on wagon wheels as opposed to bowls of fruit. And there were two real wagon wheels leaning on the stone accident-waiting-to-happen. Kindling in waiting. This place would go up in about five seconds.

The three of them began exploring their surroundings. Maricella studied the art, opened every drawer she could find, and checked out the bedrooms. Damon checked out the kitchen, and Hadji wandered out the front door. Maricella joined Damon in the kitchen, and in his rifling of the cupboards to see what they were going to have for dinner.

"I never realized Hamburger Helper had so many varieties," Maricella said. "And that they helped tuna and chicken, too. Aww, look at the little glove with the happy face on it. He looks so friendly and helpful. Well, looks like boxes and cans for a few days. At least we won't starve."

Damon checked out the freezer. "Plenty of hamburger to be helped. And yay, pizza!" He went through the fridge, checking the dates on a gallon of milk and a jug of orange juice. "It's all good. This place was recently stocked. But have you ever seen a place so generic?"

"No personal effects—nothing, nada—anywhere. As plain-brown-wrapper as they come." She looked at something out the window. "Looks like Hadji made a new friend."

Hadji came through the front door with his new friend.

"Check it—it's a minidonkey! I'm calling him Bandito. There are llamas, too, but I hear they spit. C'mon, Bandito!" They wandered back outside. Bandito followed Hadji's command.

"Well, it's someone's place," Damon said. "Someone's gotta care for the animals."

Maricella looked out the window at Hadji and Bandito. "Look at him. He's like a little kid with a new puppy. How did that creature who's been extorting half of St. Paul and hitting on me since day one suddenly become so adorable?"

"He's got a way of growing on you. One minute you want to throttle him, the next, well, you still want to throttle him, but give him a hug when you're done. I don't think he had much of a chance to be a kid."

Maricella looked around the room and sighed, then turned her attention to the back of the Hamburger Helper box. "Ever make this stuff?"

"Sure, good bachelor food. What are we having?"

"Not bourbon pork chops and mashed potatoes. Cheeseburger Macaroni do anything for you?"

"My favorite. Do we have green beans? Wax beans would be even better."

"Wax bowl of fruit on the table if you want dessert. What the hell is a wax bean? Oh wait, don't answer. I'm afraid you might actually answer the question."

"I'm sensing a high degree of sass, sister."

"You got this? You seem to be the expert here."

"Sure."

Hadji walked back in the house with Bandito in tow. He plopped down on the love seat, and Bandito stood right next to him, nudging him with his nose.

"What's for lunch?" Hadji asked. "We're hungry. Hey, think the G-men will freak if I take a spin on that tractor in the barn?"

The heavenly warmth of neurotransmission.

"Tractor?"

"Yeah," Hadji said. "It looks brand new."

"Show me."

Fifty Eight

Hadji and Bandito led the way to the barn, with Damon and Maricella bringing up the rear. Bandito was now following Hadji without command, like he had a new best friend. He seemed happy about it, too, breaking into a braying, leg-kicking donkey dance on the way to the barn. Then he got really excited and broke into a trot, taking a run at one of the llamas inside the double doors. The llama made a hissing bleat and tried to jerk out of the way of the charging minidonkey, but not before Bandito got in a minidonkey head-butt into its rear quarters. Hadji offered an explanation of his friend's behavior.

"He loves messing with that llama. Look, he's laughing."

Bandito was swaying his tail and shaking his head, and making grumbly minidonkey noises. Then he pretended like he was going to take another run at the llama, just to make him flinch. Then the cow got into the act, backing her rear end into Bandito's face, slapping it with her tail. Chickens clucked. The cow mooed. The other llama made, well, llama noises, which got the pig oinking and running around.

"Mr. Haney shows up, I'm making a break for it," Maricella said.

The faded red paint that dressed the outside of the barn turned a weathered gray on the inside. There was plentiful hay stacked in the lofts and strewn around for bedding and eating, as though it had been recently stocked and tended. The barn was damp with the March thaw, the soft breeze infused with manure and must and old iron and wood. Manure had a commanding lead. Maricella held her silk, perfumed sleeve up to her nose. Damon concentrated on breathing out of his mouth. Hadji was suddenly Farmer Bob, chewing on a twig of hay, his thumbs hooked into the straps of his imaginary overalls.

"Show you the hayloft, doll?" But he was still a Hadji.

"Want to meet that pitchfork?"

Damon tiptoed over to the tractor like he was walking through a minefield, trying to keep his loafers out of the barnyard piles that were just lying in wait for some city slicker's shoe. He made it without incident, and would worry about the return trip later.

The New Holland tractor looked fairly new to Damon's eyes, and he studied it curiously. Hadji and Maricella studied Damon's odd behavior in the same manner, which led to a look and a shrug.

"You two are starting to make my family look normal," Maricella said.

Damon stopped studying the tractor and straightened when he reached the front arm of the bucket, as though he found what he was looking for. He pulled out his wallet and fished out a card for verification:

LUCOVICH IMPLEMENT • AUTHORIZED BOBCAT DEALER
FARM AND CONSTRUCTION EQUIPMENT
SALES • PARTS • SERVICE
MASON, WISCONSIN

Verification confirmed. Which made him smile. Then he flipped the card over to look at the number Rumples scrawled on the back. *Just let me know if you see anything unusual.* Damon felt that his current situation qualified nicely.

The heavenly warmth of neurotransmission.

Damon did a cursory turn of the barn's interior before setting off toward the back of the building, where there was a walled off area adjacent to three horse stables. He once again navigated through the minefield on the balls of his feet, as though he were crossing a stream, searching for a suitable stone for each subsequent step.

His next destination came with another smile, not only for finding what he was looking for, but that his Bruno Maglis came through unmussed. He disappeared behind the walled off area and began talking to himself.

Hadji turned to Maricella. "Okay," he began, "I think Jethro's been knocked out too many times, or those scratches are all infected and turning him into a total nutjob."

"I don't know. He seems okay," Maricella said. "I mean, he's been a *little* strange since he got all scratched up, but he's a little strange to begin with. Ruh roh."

"How's that, sis?" Hadji asked.

"'Ruh roh.' Just something he said. It's either Astro from *The Jetsons* or Scooby Doo from...nevermind."

"You get scratched up, too, Cello? Maybe somewhere you can't see. I could check you out just to make sure."

"Bet that tractor makes a nice, deep hole."

"Maricella?" Damon called from the back room.

"What?"

"Telephone."

Fifty Nine

Maricella surveyed the minefield then looked down at her six-hundred dollar Emporio Armani brogues and sighed. If only she would have known she was going the *Green Acres* route, she could have picked up some shit kickers at Fleet Farm to augment her fashionista splurge at Macy's. Then Bandito got his nose up her backside and gave her a getting-to-know-you nudge. No wonder he and Hadji got along so well. But it got her moving.

She used the same stepping-stone approach as Damon did, plotting her path as she went. She held up the bottom of her Santorelli pants to keep them from dragging through the wet, soiled hay, and had to lean back for fear of being tipped over by her nudging minidonkey rudder. Bandito decided to come along for the ride. And he couldn't care less about Armani or Santorelli. Maybe he didn't like Italian designers. But he sure liked Maricella. The feeling wasn't mutual, and resulted in more unladylike language. Bandito was the Hadji of the minidonkey world.

"Heh-heh, somebody likes you," Hadji said.

"Get your donkey out of my *business.*"

"Heh-heh, businessdonkey. Good one, Cello."

"Shoo. Fetch. Squirrel!" Maricella said, trying to disengage her rudder. "Damn. Used to work every time on our golden retriever." She tried a swat across his nose.

Bandito swatted back.

With one muscular nudge, Bandito launched Maricella to the starboard side, and into a mound of hay. She landed softly enough, which ran counter to her language, which was anything but soft, and salty enough to blush a midshipman. Bandito let out a king-of-the-hill bray, then went back to making grumbly minidonkey noises and shaking his head and swaying his tail.

"Roll in the hay?" Hadji said.

"Ahhrgh!"

"Heh-heh."

Maricella got back up on her brogues and soldiered on toward the back of the barn. Bandito, having made his point with Maricella, was back hanging out with Hadji, whose focus was now trained on the tractor. He was surely planning his next round of mischief, because he was a Hadji and that's what Hadjis do. And now he had a minidonkey partner in crime. Menacing the countryside was a distinct possibility. At the very least, messing with the federal agents down the road.

A right at the stables brought Maricella into Damon's view, and a view behind the curtain where he had been keeping himself. It was a small room with an old farmhouse table sitting in the middle of it, its top red at one time, but overcome by the years and scars from all manner of farm implements being tossed on it or repaired. The floor was a gritty mix of hay stubble ground into the dirt. Damon was leaning against the table with his arms folded, a heavily soiled black handset from a wall-mounted rotary phone cradled on his shoulder.

"For you," he said, extending her the phone.

Maricella took hold of the phone with her fingertips, as though she were trying to hold a fish, and didn't really want to.

"We are so going five-star *bon vivant* as soon as we escape Hooterville," she said to Damon. She looked at the bottom of her shoe.

"God, I hate the country." She put the phone in the vicinity of her ear. "Hello?"

"Come, come, Miss Naimo. Fresh air, clean, natural living, pastoral beauty, all good for the soul."

Agent Charles.

"There is nothing *fresh* about this air. And that donkey is a pervert—you stuck us in *Green bleeping Acres*, you ass!"

"He is a rascal, at that," Charles said. "Loves sticking it to that llama. They're quite a motley crew, but it relaxes me."

"So glad your little barnyard oasis puts you in your happy fun place. But where the bleep are we and when the bleep do we get out of here?"

"The latter is easy. Sit tight for a couple of days, and you're back for the funeral. That's all there is to it. The rest of the details you can get from your brother—the one who doesn't kill people. Understood?"

"Fine."

"Why, you sound downright disheartened, Miss Naimo. Buck up, you're home in a couple days. And I'm going to give you a project to help pass the time."

"Oh God. What?"

"How many cows did you see?"

"I didn't take inventory, but I think there's only one."

"There should be two. You'll have to fetch the second."

"Excuse me? Not exactly the ropin' and wranglin' type."

"There's a small stand of trees just north of the barn. That's where she'll be. Likes to hide out there. Take some apples and coax her back to the others."

Maricella pulled the phone away from her ear and looked at it with profound disbelief. She tried it again.

"This can't be happening," she said. "What am I, the *cow whisperer*? Are you out-of-your-bleeping-mind serious?"

"I am. Damnedest thing. Think she's got some kind of social anxiety disorder, or maybe she's just afraid of being turned into steaks. Go fetch her."

She looked at the phone again, like it was some new, disturbing species. Then something dawned on her.

"Is this some kind of test?" she asked.

"Maybe. More bargaining, actually."

"Are you messing with me?"

"Oh God, yes."

"Enjoying yourself?"

"Oh saints be praised, yes."

"And if I pass the test?"

"I'll be grateful."

"Perhaps give me something in return?"

"Perhaps maybe."

"What the hell does that mean?"

"And you won't even have to roll on your brother."

"Ohhh..."

"Hop to it, cowgirl."

Sixty

Maricella hung up the phone and started shaking her head and making grumbly noises akin to smart-ass minidonkeys, except peppered with language most often associated with sailors. It was aimed at no one in particular, just some generalized steam that needed to be blown off, which she did, and she was able to reengage the here and now, which just created more steam to be released, which she did again. Rinse and repeat, and she was ready to rejoin the world.

"Gotta fetch a cow. You?"

"I think I'm good," Damon said. Then the tractor started. "Might have to look into that."

Hadji was taking a crash course in how to operate a New Holland T6030 outfitted with a backhoe and front end loader. Judging from the sporadic functions being demonstrated, Hadji was using the *wonder what this does* approach to his tractoring. In between revs of the diesel engine were the wiping of wipers, the lighting of lights, and in keeping with the true and literal spirit of the term *crash course*, were the crashing of the front and rear buckets, slamming first on the ground, then up and swinging into the wall, the teeth of the front bucket tearing a jagged gash through the old barn wood. Having mastered the operation of the joysticks and completing his remodeling project, it was time for a drive in the country. Hadji ground the gears a little more and headed for the double doors. Bandito brayed and hopped up and down, headbutted the llama again, then ran alongside Hadji to go menace the countryside.

"Good luck with your cow project, which you can explain to me later," Damon said. "There're some waders with built-in boots just around the corner. Might be more suitable to your project than Armani. I better catch up to Hadji before he takes out some buildings."

Behind the waders were a canvas barn coat and a sack of deer apples. The garments were cold and stiff and smelled like barn, but would fare much better in battle than Italian leather and linen. The boots were large enough so Maricella wouldn't have to remove her shoes, so her silk socks wouldn't be slipping and sliding inside the neoprene shells. And she liked those socks almost as much as her shoes. Maricella was as passionate about shoes as Imelda Marcos, but in a healthier, less fetishy, fascist way. At least she wasn't looting the treasury or starving her people to support her habit.

Damon and Bandito became pilot fish to Hadji's great white sharktractor. They were following alongside him wherever he went, which invariably meant that there was a lot of swerving involved. Hadji's tractoring skills were hardly adroit, and his movements were more akin to an M1 tank than a tractor. And being that most of the structures surrounding him were constructed of dried-out old wood, he might as well have been in a tank. He would go through them like a sledgehammer through a Popsicle-stick house.

"Fence!" Damon yelled.

Or like a front end loader through a wooden fence. The wall put up a better fight.

Sharktractor 2, Green Acres 0.

Maricella shrugged off the sounds of demolition and wriggled into the waders. She snugged up the suspenders as tight as they would go, barn coat over the top, work gloves conveniently tucked inside its pockets. She thought about the absurdity of what she was doing, but what the hell, there wasn't exactly a bevy of options to choose from. And the promise of any information about her father's secrets in connection with the church would make it all worthwhile. She loaded up her pockets with as many apples as they would hold and began to march.

The march was more Frankenstein's monster than foot soldier, but it got the animals to scatter as though she were the former. She waved her hand and growled just like old bolt neck for giggles, which put an extra jump in their step and a smile on her face. She was a mob girl, after all, and that was payback for putting Emporio through all the trouble.

The wooden fence that Hadji just turned into matchsticks stood as a bulwark for the woodshed. Although it failed miserably in its bulwarking duties, it provided a golden opportunity to field-test the tractor's front end loader. And Hadji passing up a golden opportunity was like a wolf passing up an elk steak. He went to work.

Hadji's gaming chops made him pretty solid on the joystick, and he proved a quick study on the loader. He backed up, dropped the bucket and engaged drive, scooping up a pile of splintered wood, although the bucket contained more earth than wood. He lifted the load and brought it over to the woodshed just like an old pro. Not so much on the stopping thing. Which he didn't, driving the teeth of the raised bucket right into the corner of the woodshed, which was like kicking a leg out on a table. At least all the wood was in one pile.

Sharktractor 3, Green Acres 0.

Maricella picked up some company as she marched toward the stand of trees that hid the bashful Hereford. They were employing the barnyard sneak approach, tiptoeing as softly as their sixteen hooves would allow, and stopping whenever Maricella stopped, perhaps thinking she was like a T. rex, and if they didn't move, she couldn't see them. Perhaps a fatal flaw in logic that found them more often than not as a dinner entrée. But they were keeping a healthy distance from the crazy lady in the extra-large waders, just in case she growled at them again. Of course they were just begging to be messed with, and Maricella was happy to oblige.

You don't mess with a mob girl's shoes.

Sixty One

Here we come
Walking down the street
We get the funniest looks from
Everyone we meet

The funniest looks came courtesy of the federal agents down the road, but they were aimed at each other, as opposed to the surreality that kindled them, which was fast approaching. To be specific, one was jogging, one was trotting, and one was driving a great white sharktractor, its teeth bared and raised and trained on their government-issued ass. And it was driven by a Hadji, who still didn't quite have the hang of the whole stopping thing, which didn't seem to bother him all that much. It was accompanied by shouting, occasional braying, and, to be sure, some mischievous laughter that couldn't be heard by the outside world.

Heh-heh.

There was another party walking down another street, also sharing universal funny looks amongst themselves. They were a motley mix of barnyard and shit-kicking mob girl, on a search-and-rescue mission for a bashful Hereford. To wit: One cow, two llamas, and a pig bringing up the rear, led by the aforementioned manure punter with a penchant for Italian haute couture. No wonder the chickens chose to sit this one out.

The Quantico twins were trying to play it cool, and they certainly looked the part. Matching dark suits and overcoats, close-cropped hair cropped too close to part, peering out from their sunglasses at a scenario that was probably not on the training docket at the FBI Academy. They held out twin universal stop signs to halt the onrushing insurgents, reemphasizing their command by boldly stepping forward, as if to say *we really mean it this time*, which doesn't even work on little kids. Its odds of working on a Hadji in a great white sharktractor, already with a pure hat trick in the bag and on the power play again?

Cue the fat lady.

The shit-kicking mob girl party arrived at the site of their quarry, a jumble of mixed trees jutting out of the prairie landscape like an island in the sea. The island had one inhabitant, a reddish brown cow with a white face and markings, chewing its cud while looking at the goings-on of the great white sharktractor, like it was just having dinner and staring blankly at the TV, which, despite its English heritage, made it like every other American. It assimilated nicely. Maricella took a stab at some conversation.

"Hey, little doggie, want a treat? C'mere, girl." It was Maricella's first conversation with a cow. The old cowboy song "Whoopie Ti Yi Yo" was the first reference that came to mind, so that's what she went with. She pulled out a couple of apples and stepped into the trees toward the bashful Hereford. The cow seemed agreeable to the idea, and took a step in her direction.

The others in her party liked the idea, too. Suddenly, she found herself in the middle of a barnyard rugby scrum, and she had the ball. The oft head-butted llama was the pushiest, nosing at her pocketful of apples, then putting some teeth into the effort, which found some skin.

"Hey! That hurt!" Maricella said. "No wonder that pervert donkey doesn't like you." The other llama made it a double-team effort. The other cow was nosing in, and the pig scurried and oinked, perhaps in protest of the height differential.

"I knew it. You're nothing but a bunch of barnyard mercenaries. Damon!"

Damon already had his hands full. Actually, more tied than full, because there wasn't much he could do but yell at Hadji, who wasn't hearing any of it. He and Bandito were at ramming speed.

"He doesn't know how to stop!" Damon yelled at the Quantico twins. "Run!"

So they did. With a charging minidonkey on their tail. Hadji stopped like he usually did.

Sharktractor 4, Green Acres 0.

Sixty Two

The Quantico twins went from cool to bumbling to straight into Rod Serling's wheelhouse inside a minute. They were being held at bay by a head-butting minidonkey who wouldn't let them pass, and could only watch helplessly as their government-issued vehicle was being taken apart like the *Orca* was in *Jaws*. Extrication from the mortally wounded Suburban was a tad messy, as the toothy shark-tractor was shaking its prey around, as was its evolutional nature. But Hadji worked his way free, and deeming the countryside sufficiently menaced, headed for the barn. Bandito released his prisoners and trotted off to join him. Leaving in their collective wake two gape-mouthed federal agents with a lot of explaining to do, and a government vehicle with a really bad haircut.

Maricella had extrication issues of her own. Another sharp nip from the pushy llama had pushed her to the limit, and drastic measures were required.

The Hail Mary.

Maricella broke free from the rules of barnyard rugby and dropped back *American style*, heaving a handful of apples downfield. Her barnyard receiving corps scrambled and broke deep, although their version of going deep was more reminiscent of magnetic football players from those 1970s games, where every player just ran into each other before ending up in a vibrating scrum in the middle of the field, usually with one poor schmoe off in the corner, vibrating by himself, which was disturbingly weird, enough to make Dr. Freud stroke his beard and head for the coca cabinet. Playing the role of poor schmoe in this case was the pig, who was toppled on his side during the melee, struggling to right himself while oinking his displeasure at his predicament. Weirdness of a whole nother level. Sigmund might want to make it a double.

Damon decided against playing diplomatic liaison between Hadji and the federal agents, mostly because he didn't know where to begin. The best he could do was a *what are ya gonna do?* shrug before joining Maricella for some cow whispering.

"How's the cow project coming along?" Damon asked.

"It's all about the apples around here." Maricella nodded toward the Quantico twins. "Dinner's gonna be fun with those two."

"Oh my, that's right. Suspect that barn phone will be ringing off the—" The phone started ringing. "Nevermind."

Maricella looked toward the sharktractor and Bandito. They were on approach to the barn, which, if it were not an inanimate object, would be quaking in its boots, or foundation, as it were. "How do you suppose that's going to go, Mr. Wizard?"

"I'm guessing not well. Again with the sass..."

Maricella smiled and held out an apple for the bashful Hereford. It munched it up in a few bites, and then nosed in for another. She held out another, taking a few steps out of the trees. The cow followed, as did momentum. Soon all three were heading toward the barn.

"Rumples put you up to this?" Damon asked.

"Uh-huh."

"Promise of information?"

"Also uh-huh. FBI and the families, always negotiating. Sure there's some general just-messing-with-me in there as well."

"Trust him?"

"As far as I can throw this cow."

"Reasoning?"

"Can't hurt."

"Uh-huh."

"You mocking me?"

"Brace yourself for some guff. Hey, listen—"

Hadji and Bandito had disappeared into the barn. It was quiet, and the barn was still standing. Then Bandito came charging out of the barn, on a beeline toward his favorite target. He connected a solid head-butt into its rear quarters, forcing out a honking bleat, then gobbled up his apples.

"He really doesn't like that dude," Maricella said.

"He's the Hadji of the animal world," Damon said. "Probably extorting apples from all these guys when he's not out pillaging the countryside."

Having landed the bashful Hereford to the safety of the miraculously still-standing barn, Maricella was finally free to wriggle out of her crazy-lady waders. And in thanks to the barnyard gods, she spread out a generous supply of apples for everyone, and soon all the barnyard inhabitants were contentedly munching away together. At last, peace in the valley. The sharktractor was at rest and, in yet another miracle, nicely parked, right where Hadji had found it. There was a new oddly-shaped window next to it, but the cross- ventilation was most welcome. And the phone had stopped ringing. The birds could once again be heard singing their spring calls. Peace. Cease fire.

Fire in the hole.

The explosion rocked the barn and made everyone duck in a perfectly choreographed motion. Government Suburbans blow up real good. Good enough to bring Hadji out of the back room, the handset of the phone damped against his chest. He un-damped it to check if there was a reaction from the rumply person on the other end. There was, and it could be heard on the other side of the barn. Probably the next county. Hadji, the gift that keeps on giving.

"Mighta nicked the gas line."

Sixty Three

Dinner conversation was a bit on the icy side, which did little to cool the complexions of the Quantico twins, which were still running north of florid. They were glowering at Hadji with so much intensity that, if they had cartoon bubbles, you'd see Hadji in a large black cauldron, simmering away à la Looney Tunes. Luckily, Hadjis are great ice breakers, which does little to make up for their lack of timing.

"Sorry about your ride, boys. My bad. It was an accident."

Their next cartoon bubble had steam blowing from their ears, which makes speaking difficult, even more so when coupled with clenched teeth. But they tried, professionals that they were. Tones just north of agitated Clint Eastwood.

"Two words," QT1 said. "Totem Town."

"Two more," QT2 said. "Long time."

"Boys been married long?"

That timing thing is a tricky devil.

They both shot up from the table. Damon held out the stop sign, forced into the role of diplomatic liaison.

"Gentlemen, please," Damon said, trying to lure them back in their seats with a guiding hand. "Full reparations and restitution will

180　•　PERRY ANTHONY

be made via Agent Charles. I'll see to it personally."

Hadji's next words were squelched by Maricella's index finger, which indicated that class was in session again. It worked. Then Bandito head-butted open the front door and just stood there, like he just got up in his corner, ready for Round Two.

"God bless America," Maricella said.

"Spose he's going to donkey jail."

Well, it worked for about ten seconds.

Cartoon bubble number three had their heads turning into steam whistles, blowing full bore. They both shared the countenance of freshly boiled lobster, and their heads looked ready to fly off. Phones started buzzing and chiming from their pockets, which did little to bring down their blood pressure. They both got up to tend to business, which mostly consisted of them listening, mostly with closed eyes aimed skyward, clearly not enjoying what they were hearing. They were, to be sure, being issued orders, and probably being told what bumbling incompetents they were. They had little to stand on in arguing the points. They wrapped things up and prepared to make their statements. The very essence of brevity.

"We're out of here first thing in the morning," QT1 said, then he and his partner retired for the evening, heading off to one of the bedrooms.

"Now no foolin' around you two," Hadji said.

"You really need to learn to play better with others," Damon said.

"Rock 'n' roll 'em as I see 'em, Jethro. C'mere, boy!"

Bandito strutted into the room, gave Hadji a nudge, then went to work on what was left of the Quantico twins' dinner, which, for some reason, was mostly untouched. QT1 reentered the room with a message for Damon.

"Agent Charles would like a word, Mr. Ramp. Be at the barn phone at seven-thirty."

"Thank you, agent—I never did catch your name."

"Might as well be mud." He left the room.

"Sounds a bit dejected," Maricella said.

"Wonder why," Damon said. They both looked at Hadji.

"Oh waah, our nation's finest just got done in by a kid and a donkey. Ain't sheddin' a tear for the fuzz."

"Fuzz?" Damon said. "You really need to stay away from that time machine. They haven't been called that since 1970. On a *Dragnet* episode. Did you come from a nearby planet?"

"Damn, there he goes again, sis," Hadji said. "Pretty soon he's just going to be walking around with a microphone and a little PA, ready to do stand-up at the drop of a hat."

"As long as it's somewhere far, far away from here," Maricella said, going away briefly before returning on the round trip. "Crap."

"That sounded like a cold realization, slap-in-the-face kind of 'crap,' sister," Damon said.

"It certainly was," Maricella said. "We're not going home, he's just moving us before we burn down his house."

"One way to find out," Damon said, motioning toward the front door.

"To the Batpoles!" Hadji said, tearing out the door, four cloppity minihooves right on his heels.

"Got the keys?" Maricella asked.

"Oh. I—" The tractor started.

"Might have to look into that?" Maricella said.

"Something like that."

Sixty Four

Keeping with its evolutional nature, the great white sharktractor was revisiting the carcass from its previous kill, just to make sure it didn't miss anything. Also in the making-sure-it-didn't-miss-anything department were the Quantico twins, the echoing screak of twisting metal beguiling them like a Siren, bringing them out from behind the curtains. They looked, listened, and wisely chose to close the curtains. They weren't about to fall for the old banana in the tailpipe twice in one evening.

Also in the looking-and-listening department was Damon. The looking part was the same as the Quantico twins, albeit from the vantage point of the barn. The listening part was a whole nother matter.

"Please tell me that's not my tractor I hear in the background. Lie if you have to."

"It's just the wind," Damon said.

"Nice. And my agents are doing what about it?"

"Putting up a valiant stand against a formidable force."

"Again, nice. Getting their ass kicked from here to Sunday?"

"Pretty much."

"They're hiding, aren't they?"

"It's just the wind."

"Refresh me, then remind me I am in a conscious state: We've got a teen in a tractor, aided and abetted by a donkey, correct?"

"Correct."

"Taking out an eighty grand government vehicle, which I'm told is a total loss, still with me?"

"Correct."

"Anything else I should know about? Don't hold back—the Vicodin and Dewar's have finally kicked in."

"Isn't that dangerous?"

"An unmedicated me is substantially more dangerous at this point."

"Okay then. Barn has a new window and the fence is down, but it's all piled up where the woodshed used to stand."

"*Used* to?"

"It's kind of sitting now."

"House still, ah, upright?"

"It is. Yay?"

"So this is what we're gonna do. Dumb and Dumber's relief will be there first thing tomorrow. Keep the wrecking ball away from my house. Capiche?"

"We're staying?"

"I got bodies dropping like flies all over the place down here. Goddam right you're staying."

"Update me."

"Christ, the hitmen are getting hit. Maybe they're gettin' it all out of their system so they can all play nice at church."

"Sniper in the tower got it, too?"

"Two A-list hitters down, one an import from the old country. Then your brother's other guy got their guy. Score's even-up with a couple of periods to go. Cowgirl there?"

"Sure," Damon said, handing the phone off to Maricella.

"Hello, room service?" Maricella said.

"Cheeky," Rumples said. "Fetch my girl?"

"Fetched and back in the barn. Satisfied?"

"Best thing that happened to me all day."

"When's payday?"

"We'll talk when this is all over—if we all make it to the end. Catch the chat I just had with your nice brother?"

"I did."

"Any light to be shed?"

"None, as long as the two principals are still in play. Any change in status there?"

"None."

"Then sorry, fresh out of light. This thing's going right down to the wire, and there are no ties in this league."

"Kids say the darndest things."

The screaks in the night had turned into out-and-out howling. The charred frame of the Suburban was pinned in the clutches of the sharktractor's toothy bucket, extended as high as it would go, the skeleton almost standing on end, looking like a mechanized monster from a bad Japanese sci-fi movie. It was slowly and screechily being folded in half.

"Wow. That's pretty impressive," Damon said, to no one in particular.

"What the hell is that *NOISE*?" Rumples shouted, loud enough to echo in the barn.

"Just tell him it's the wind," Damon said.

"Sorry. Hamburger Helper gives me the winds something awful," Maricella said into the phone.

"Close enough," Damon said.

"Agent Charles?" There was no reply. But there were sounds. Crashing sounds. With a side of screaming. "I think we made him mad again," Maricella said to Damon.

"You just can't take us anywhere."

Sixty Five

amon was right for the next thirty-six hours.
You just can't take us anywhere.

Thirty-six hours of extreme limbo with all the trimmings. No TV, radio, or phone. Not a book, magazine, or newspaper in sight. Board games? Zip. A lousy deck of cards? Nope. Nada. Zilch. El zero. There was a box of All Bran that got passed around the kitchen table in the morning, but it lacked the pizzazz of a box of Cap'n Crunch or Fruity Pebbles, and reading about fiber was about as exciting as ingesting it. At least *Gilligan's Island* had a radio and occasional visitors, and they got to leave their huts.

The new and improved version of the Quantico twins came with much more specific orders and standards. First order of business was to put the sharktractor *out* of business, so the tractor keys were the first to go. And being in the general area, might as well put the phone out of business, too. Done and done. Not surprisingly, the orders seemed prioritized and had a certain *rumply* quality about them. Also not surprisingly being as Damon, Maricella, and Hadji had a hand in driving Special Agent William Charles to drink. Drugs too. No wonder. They turned his happy fun place into a war zone. And corrupted his minidonkey. Of course it could be argued that the latter was *fait accompli*. Bandito was a bad seed if there ever was one. There probably was a series of *666*s somewhere on his minidonkey scalp.

Although it wasn't stated explicitly, circumstances implied that if the occupants of Green Acres wanted some conversation, it would have to be amongst themselves. And if they wanted to go the Dr. Dolittle route, it would have to be the telepathic version, because everyone was grounded, and they *really* meant it this time. Even the animals were under barn arrest. Version 2.0 of the Quantico twins had more Gestapo than the first one. And for thirty-six hours they camped right outside the front door, probably polishing up their jackboots while whistling Bavarian folk songs and dreaming of strudel.

It was thirty-six hours of extreme thoughts due to extreme boredom. Thirty-six hours of way too much familiarity that teetered on the borders of stark raving mad. It was an age-old malady that went by many names: *Cabin fever. Stir crazy. Climbing the walls. Shack happy.* Jack Torrance had it, and it made him an extremely dull boy with a sudden interest in lumberjacking and scenery chewing. If it weren't for the Hamburger Helper and green beans, there might have been cannibalism. And they came pretty damn close, but that was due more to an annoying game of charades than it was hunger.

There were basically three options for the happy occupants of Green Acres. They could eat, they could talk, or they could sleep. Hadji had a fourth option in mind, but Maricella would have none of it, simply reminding him of the pitchfork and the tractor's ability in making a nice, deep hole. So they ate all the food, got totally sick of each other, and tried to sleep.

And tried not to kill each other.

Sixty Six

Damon was up early in anticipation of the wake-up call. Since there was no phone to convey the message, a more primitive method was used, but with no appreciable loss in the results department. *Knock knock knock.* They were unexpectedly gentle knocks, in fact, downright polite. Damon was expecting something a little north of overzealous, perhaps something with a stern Teutonic accent demanding order and a roll call. Expected Gestapo, got Sergeant Schultz. Nice. Maybe get LeBeau to whip them up a little strudel.

"Maricella?" Damon whispered, patting her shoulder. "Guess what time it is?"

There was an initial crankiness on Maricella's part, perhaps due in part that she had been curled up on a lumpy, musty loveseat from 1973 that had been treated with a barnyard air freshener. But the crankiness passed quickly, because she knew *exactly* what time it was. A joyful smile arrived on her face to indicate it.

"Time to go home?" she said.

"Hotel San Pablo sound okay?" Damon said.

"Home of poofy towels and robes and Jacuzzi tubs and yummy room service?"

"Or we could stay at my place. Hamburger Helper and wax beans in the cupboard."

"They say your first answer is always your best one. Let's stick with that. And if you take me to the country again I'll bury you with that backhoe. Capiche?"

"Capiche."

"Hey, Hadji," Damon said, nudging him with his foot. "You still with us?"

Hadji wriggled around on the bearskin rug and stretched out his arms and legs. Kind of just like a dog. "Crap," he said.

"Most people go with 'good morning,'" Damon said.

"You try sleeping on a rug, Jethro. It's like I'm your freaking dog." Guess he kind of felt like one, too.

"Need to go out, boy?" Damon asked.

"Cello? I swear, he's turning into a complete nutjob. Go see a freakin' doctor, you wacko," he said to Damon.

"Heh-heh," Damon said.

There was a sudden commotion outside the front door. One of the Gestapo twins yelled "Get away from me!" The other yelped "Ow!" It was followed by massive, echoing thuds, that sounded like someone kicking a government Suburban. Three heads scrunched together at the window to confirm it.

Bandito had commenced with Round Two. And he was kicking the shit out of said Suburban.

"Wow. Check the torque on that dude!" Hadji said, in admiration of his four-legged partner in crime. Bandito was whaling on the passenger side doors with his two back legs. Total donkey style. And doing incredible damage. The Gestapo twins looked as helpless as the Quantico pair. One of them fired his service weapon into the air to try and stop him. Bandito tore after him like a bat out of hell. All the way down the road.

"Please tell me he's not the one with the keys," Maricella said.

"Anything for you, doll," Hadji said. Men. Mornings. Lumber.

"Pitchfork. Backhoe."

"Buzzkill."

Gestapo twin number one returned from his morning jog looking a little worse for wear, and with even less to say. Being outsmarted and bitchslapped by the minidonkey spawn of Satan will do that to you. His crisp suit was no longer, his tie was twisted like someone tried to strangle him with it, and his white shirt was anything but. His dirty face was smeared like it was ready for a nighttime ambush. And he was the one with the keys, which he pulled out of his pocket without a word and crawled into the cockpit of the government Suburban, that kind of looked like he did. Bandito, like Hadji, the gift that keeps on giving. True kindred spirits.

And it was time to say good-bye. Somewhere, Vera Lynn was singing.

We'll meet again,
don't know where, don't know when
But I know we'll meet again some sunny day

Sixty Seven

Three hours to kill on the road with the Gestapo twins as your pilot and co-pilot was about as pleasant as a full cavity search. Three hours to kill on the road with Damon, Maricella, and Hadji in their present states was a close second.

The last thirty-six hours had them at the teetering edge of shack-happy Jack Torrance territory. They were practically begging for the Mickey-laced sleeping masks to come out. And when you've done nothing but try to sleep for the last thirty-six hours, cooped up with the same damn two other people, you start seeing Jack Nicholson gimping around with an ax, and perhaps thinking that it may not be such a bad idea.

Or you could play car games.

Although it probably was ill-advised, considering their last game of charades almost ended in capital murder, something had to be done to kill the boredom of the road. They started out with Counting Cows, a good game considering they were in the Dairy State. Damon added bonus points for the Dutch Belted variety, which garnered you-are-so-weird looks from Hadji and Maricella, who, at last, finally agreed on something. Damon somewhat redeemed himself when he described that variety of cow as an Oreo cookie on four legs, bolstering his comeback even more by adding the rule that you had to say "Oreo cow" when you spotted one. Of course this also bolstered Hadji's case that Damon was cracking up and turning into a total nutjob. Counting Deer was too exhausting, which was akin to counting squirrels in the suburbs. The best one was Counting Turkeys, because you had to gobble when you saw a wild turkey. This was Hadji's favorite because it made Gestapo twin No. 1 want to snap off the steering wheel. And being a Hadji, he cheated just to drive him nuts, placing the gobbles—in several twisted variations—right into his ear. The German accented gobble almost landed them in the ditch. *Der gobble*. The CIA never would have had to resort to waterboarding if they had a Hadji.

When they laughed it had a hysterical tinge to it. Slug Bug escalated into a slapfest with the appearance of the first, and thankfully last, Volkswagen. The last thirty-six hours really had done a number on them. They got closer to normal when they spotted the big 1ˢᵗ on the First National Bank building, *closer* and *normal* being relative terms at this point. The sun did its best to help out, trying to shake off the March overcast. Seeing the Hotel San Pablo got them a little closer. Reginald took them the rest of the way.

The large black man with the thick goatee and Rasta accent, resplendent in his scarlet vest and top hat and tails, was graciously manning his post. His hands were open, his arms spread wide in welcome, his smile bright as spring sunshine.

"Miss Maricella and Mr. Damon!" Reginald said with a bouncing lilt. "So good to have you home. Welcome..." He bowed and gestured them inside with a guiding hand.

"What it is, Jim!" Hadji said, holding out his palm for Reginald to slap it.

"Okay. Pretty sure no one's heard that since *What's Happening*," Damon said to Hadji. "How many times do I have to tell you, *stay away from the time machine.*"

"Workin' the Improv tonight, Jethro? *Wacko.*"

"Ah, the young squire, Hootie," Reginald said. The words sounded nice. The look looked like a hammer ready to drive home a nail.

"It's Hadji," Hadji said. "Not seein' any Blowfish here, Jim."

"Jah guide, young squire. Now move yu backside."

"Phone call, Mr. Ramp," a bellman said.

An alert was issued to all hotel personnel: *Phone call guy's back.*

"Hello?"

"Ah, back to civilization, Mr. Ramp," Rumples said. "Another day, another government vehicle totaled...another pair of ashamed agents. CIA could have used you three at Guantanamo. House still standing?"

"Did you buy that donkey directly from Satan?" Damon asked.

"Catch myself asking the same. Did he really put the boots to that truck?"

"The torque was pretty impressive. The chase after was even better. You have very fit agents."

"I'd take a little less brawn if I could have a little more brain," Rumples said. "Donkeys shouldn't be getting the upper hand rumbling with the FBI. That little bastard is a handful, though."

"Big day tomorrow."

"Oh boy."

Two simple one-syllable words never conveyed such complexity and nuance, exhaustion and worry. Comprehension of a thousand details. Nothing but careers and life and death on the line. Rumples's *Oh boy* had about a million miles on it.

"Last mile," Damon said.

"Long sonofabitch."

Sixty Eight

Damon was up with the sun Friday morning, well-rested and crisp, his brain taut and ready to run, like a Ferrari V12 at fast idle. He loved it when he felt this way, his whole body seeming to hum, all circuits on, on his A-game, ready to rock 'n' roll. His brain was streaming data from all sectors and their respective files, flowing as freely as a wide open faucet, with the snap of a fresh deck of cards on a clean shuffle. He got a quick cup of coffee in him, but needed to walk and think fast, his brain craving exercise and complexity. The weather on the last Friday in March was in perfect step, crisp and clear, more fall-like than spring, the northern air dry instead of southerly soft. A cool fifty-one degrees, but relatively warm after nearly five months of winter.

Damon speed-walked around the Rice Park District, accompanying his steps with simple calculations, ramping up to Euclid's algorithm as he went up and around Market Street to West Fifth, St. Peter to West Fourth, looping the hotel but continuing down Fourth to Washington Street, past the St. Paul Central Library and Ordway Center, completing the roundabout circle back at Market. He was fittingly engulfed in the random walk hypothesis by the time he closed the circle. Which was nothing but a meandering theoretical exercise that ended up at the conclusion that some things are completely random. Forrest Gump had it at *shit happens.*

Damon returned to the room to find Maricella in a totally different state. She was in her A-game zone as well, but her game looked and worked a lot different than Damon's. Behind her wide brown eyes was virtually no activity, just an open, clear receptacle on high alert. Mind clear and uncluttered, eyes open, head on a swivel, ears like highly sensitive microphones, as though she were a soldier on point. She was quiet and she wasn't hungry, there was no room service in the room, nor did she suggest that they go downstairs to eat breakfast at the café. Zero appetite. She was freshly showered and working on coffee. Both on top of their respective games, night and day in methods of operation.

Damon wasn't accustomed to getting the dialogue rolling. He spent most of his life in the role of counterpuncher, i.e., speak when you're spoken to. But somebody had to say something eventually. Plus, he was craving logistical information. He needed to know what his day was going to look like so he could prepare.

"How are you doing?" he said. Simple, but it came with the sweetness of genuine concern.

"I'm in a million knots. This is going to be a really long day, so bear with me."

"I'm at your beck and call, sister."

Maricella said *thank you* with a look. Damon received the message so clearly he nearly said *you're welcome* aloud. "Going with the Armani?" she asked. A step closer to normal.

Slim-fit combed wool. Black on black. Dark blue jacquard silk tie over a Van Heusen pearl shirt. Bruno Magli tie-up oxfords.

"Oh boy."

"Have to beat 'em off with a stick," Maricella said. Another step.

"If only I didn't look like *I've* been beaten with a stick."

"We could try some concealer."

"Don't bother. I've gotten used to the fact that my face is a conversation piece. Someone's gonna have to amuse the mourning Guidos."

"Guido doesn't mourn as much as pay his respects," Maricella said. "It's a relatively brief process. Wait till the reception here after the funeral—you'd be hard-pressed to tell if you were at a wedding or a funeral."

"Speaking of which...how are we doing this?"

"I spoke with Antonio while you were out. We're doing this separately, okay?"

"I understand," Damon said. And he did. It made perfect sense, and it was his preference. This would allow him to concentrate on the goings-on at the funeral, and allow Maricella time to grieve and be with her family.

"We'll catch up at the reception. I'll introduce you to Uncle Rigo."

"The sweet, little old Italian man that's kind of short and ro-ly-poly from too many raviolis?"

"The one and only."

"Does he have anything to do with the business end of the family?" Damon asked.

"To tell you the truth, I've never been totally sure, but I don't think so. If he does, it's with an invisible hand."

"Which wouldn't be too unusual, would it?"

"I guess not. But it's not like there's some kind of organizational flowchart to confirm it. What are you thinking?"

"Just want to know all the players on the roster."

"You got a look." Maricella's head tilted in curiosity. "Like an eagle. Like nothing's getting past you today."

"Today, I settle all family business." Damon held the grave face for a beat, then started laughing. "I've been practicing my Michael Corleone. How'd I do?"

"Hadji may be on to something. Now you're doing imperson-ations."

"Irie, where is the young squire, Hootie?"

"Okay, okay, you can stop now, I feel better," Maricella said. "Thank you."

"You're welcome."

"Come to think of it, he has kind of disappeared, hasn't he? Suppose he's up to something?"

"Of course he's up to something. He's a Hadji."

Sixty Nine

The balcony of a little French church, to be exact.

Reparations had begun in earnest between Hadji and Rumples, the latter not getting where he was today for failing to snag a big, fat opportunity when presented. To wit: Hadji could go where the FBI couldn't, as the aforementioned church took great umbrage at the notion of having a house of God wired for sight and sound, unmoved by the argument that their houseguests for the day might have broken a commandment or two, and probably wouldn't pay attention to their NO GUNS ALLOWED ON PREMISES sign. Matter of principle. So if you can't get in the front door, you go around to the back, where you usually find guys like Hadji, who could probably offer up some pointers to federal agencies when it came to furtive surveilling. And he really enjoyed his work. Also he wasn't encumbered in the least by any ethical or moral standards, or pesky constitutional amendments. In other words, he was perfect.

So was Maricella.

Elegance personified in a black capped-sleeve belted dress, violet sapphire earrings, necklace and bracelet in white gold, black Giorgio Armani square-toe pumps for kicks. Conservative, appropriate, yet sufficiently devastating. She really enjoyed her work, too, as her day job consisted of her being rich, and shopping with no limits is definitely top ten in wonders of the world.

"A million knots never looked so good," Damon said.

"Thank you, Damon. You always make me feel better. You're a good brother. The other one's a little more complicated."

Damon saw the complications as much as he felt them, because they were written all over Maricella. Beyond the beauty were eyes of distance and depth, the lines around them tight. Her body rigid and tense, brow unconsciously furrowed. She really was in a million knots.

"What did Antonio tell you?"

She didn't answer right away. Or at all. She just looked at Damon.

"That bad?"

"Keep those eagle eyes wide open," Maricella finally spoke. "This thing is white hot and ready to flash."

Damon knew it. He felt it. That's why all his circuits were full throttle.

"Pashtun doesn't care if it's a funeral," Damon said. "He only cares about opportunity. Why don't—nevermind, I—"

"Did that one all by yourself." Maricella finally cracked a smile. "But I'll explain anyway. Cancel the funeral? This is going to happen, funeral or no. Antonio sees opportunity as much as Pashtun does. In fact, that's what he's betting on."

"That his guys see Pashtun's first."

"Now take in the lay of the land," Maricella said.

Damon had already begun before she even finished her sentence. His probability-correlations file was winnowing out scenarios, his geography profiles feeding the PC file logistical data. Floor plans, arterial streets, routes, bushes, traffic, buildings. Throw in a light-rail train coming right down Broadway to boot. Snipes in the towers ruled out first, they'll be covered like a blanket.

"It's coming up close and personal," Damon said. "Like a whisper." Then he tilted like a pinball machine. Total system crash. "Shit! I can't get a read. It's like trying to pick a zebra out of a pack of zebras."

"I think it's 'herd,'" Maricella said, amused at Damon's processes, smiling a little wider at the opportunity of providing Damon with some extraneous Damonesque information. "Actually, 'zeal' is more accurate, but you won't get thrown out of the classroom if you refer to them as a 'dazzle' of zebras." She enjoyed the moment for a beat. "More germane to the current, which guy in a suit with a gun? In a business rife with traitors and double-crosses. Run that one around in your brain for a while. It's bleeping 'Where's Waldo'—but you don't know if Waldo is the real Waldo. And some-body swore-er..."

"Nice. Guff and sass, added bonus for arcane reference. But now my head hurts."

"Goes nicely with your face. Such a nice face."

"Irie! Jah guide!"

"Don't know if the good Lord wants any part of this one," Maricella said.

"Good point. Did I just channel a Rasta guy? And I only swear when my head hurts. Oh, and winter hiking—that's when I pull out the good stuff."

"It's okay, you just need a vacation."

"When this is all done. Promise?"

"Promise."

"You're a nice sister."

"I know."

The phone rang. Damon and Maricella looked at it. Then each other. Exchanged about a thousand words with the look.

"Showtime."

Seventy

Revolvers are bulky. Really wreck the line of a nice slim-fit suit. Probably why semiautos gained such widespread acceptance, on account of they're flatteringly slimming. Bonus for packing more ammo.

The Great Damonico, ponderer of all things ponderous, was toying with that very notion as he tried to pack a Smith & Wesson Model 586 .357 Magnum into his Armani suit, so it wouldn't look like he was carrying around an ice cream scoop in his inside pocket. The side pockets of his jacket were only wide enough to accommodate a fashionable four-finger dip, and trying to use the pants pockets made it look like he was carrying around an armadillo, which might curry some favor with the ladies, but that's a digression of a different color. A shoulder holster would have helped seat the gun and distribute the weight better, but it still would have looked like he was carrying around a toolbox in his pocket. There also was the fact that he was somewhat preoccupied at the time he was firearms shopping, so he didn't get a chance to properly accessorize. All digressions aside, it was a helluva piece of iron. If only he had a place to put it.

Damon really hadn't given much thought as to why he wanted to bring the gun, only that he thought it might come in handy, since people might be getting killed where he was going. Like it's winter, might want to grab a hanky before you head out the door. In this case, no hanky, just a gun, and the Burberry trench provided better wiggle room in concealing its bulk, looked good in doing it, too. It certainly helped, although there was a list to the starboard side, which gave him an unwelcome droop and made him wish he would have selected a smaller gun, perhaps something along the lines of a dainty Derringer. Of course, Derringers just don't pack the punch, literally or aesthetically, of a Magnum. Aw, such a cute little gun, like you're looking at a damn puppy. More digressions aside, he needed some ballast. A glass ashtray would have been about right, but carrying one concealed might get you into more trouble than carrying a gun. But the Swingline 767 on the desk just might right the ship. A once-over in the mirror confirmed it. A mental once-over and a pat to confirm drove home the fact that the gun was on his right. Don't want to be bringing no stapler to a gunfight.

Strolling through the lobby of a grand hotel dressed to the nines has a certain *je ne sais quoi*, and Damon would have been walking on air if only he weren't weighed down by a gun and a stapler, and had a face that was beginning to resemble the stitch-marked goalie mask that Gerry Cheevers wore with the Boston Bruins, circa 1970. Gravity's a bitch. But the Brunos and Armani felt fine, and the Smith added a touch of badass. Take that, gravity. Also of note was, well, a note that was being waved at Damon as he passed the concierge's desk.

"For you, Mr. Ramp," the nice lady at the desk said. She was trying really hard not to stare at Damon's face. So much so that the effort was more conspicuous than the staring would have been. Damon let it go and read the note:

> SO WE CAN KEEP EACH OTHER IN THE LOOP. HIT
> 2 AND SEND TO SPEED DIAL ME. HOLD STAR KEY 3
> TICKS TO PUT ON VIBRATE. GET BORED IN CHURCH
> GO TO PICTURES. NOW HOLD OUT YOUR HAND SO
> THE NICE LADY CAN GIVE YOU SOMETHING. HADJI.

Damon looked up at the nice lady, who had been joined by a few of her staff, who were waving more staff over, like it was time for a team meeting.

"For you, Mr. Ramp," the nice lady said, now standing, an air of ceremony about her.

She raised her chin and extended her arms, her hands together as if in prayer. Then came the dramatic pause, which, combined with the gun and the stapler, made Damon feel like a contestant on *Let's Make A Deal.* And nice lady Carol Merrill was milking it like a damn Holstein, the thought of which made Damon grin, because somewhere deep in his repository of innocuous facts was the nugget that Carol Merrill was not only from Frederic, Wisconsin, but she spent the first ten years of her life growing up on a farm. Symmetric perfection at 360°.

Now open the damn curtain already.

Which she did. Very, very slowly. *The Gift of the Magi* had less drama.

And there it was. The prayered hands open in magnanimity, a gift to the world...for the beneficence of mankind...*Kumbaya, my Lord—*

A flip phone.

But it was followed by a nice round of applause from the hotel staff. Guess he did have a few too many calls.

Damon thought of doing something untoward with the Swing-line, but his better angels intervened and he politely said thank you instead, and flipped open his new phone—well, new being a relative term, because Damon, although no technophile, was pretty sure that phones hadn't *flipped* in a while. Hadji had been messing with the time machine again. He found him a damn flip phone. Might as well see if it works. He pressed 2.

"Heh-heh. Cool phone, dude."

"Couldn't find a rotary model?"

"Trust me, Jethro, it's you. Where you at?"

"Just about to pass your friend, Jim. Tell 'im Hootie says hi?"

"Doing a set at Yuk Yuks after church? *Wacko.*"

"Where you at?"

"Hangin' around the hive. Dish looks ferosh. Hubba hubba."

"Okay. I'm going to try and translate," Damon began. "Hive, buzzing with activity, I'm going 'church'—which I'm guessing you've got wired up to eleven."

"Correctamundo."

"BTW, for the FBI?"

"Bonus. Style points for the BTW—take it to the house hilly-billy."

"Pitchfork. Backhoe. Familiar?"

"Heh-heh."

"Tell me what you're seeing."

"Seeing a lot of shiny suits and pinky rings—and someone forgot to tell Guido about smoking, 'cause they're all huffin' like chimneys out on the steps," Hadji said. "Best part is the trains going by. All packed to the rafters with rubes, fat faces pressed up against the glass like they're at fucking Sea World—probably buy T-shirts if they could find 'em. Sat trucks everywhere. Betty Reporter lookin' fine..."

"How's the inside look?"

"Creepy old dude in a casket on display, guys in white robes prepping and talkin' to the Chief. Cello and some sharp-dressed dudes, some old fat guy waddling around like he's lookin' for a fucking sandwich."

"Uncle Rigo."

"More like Uncle Fatgo, but whatevs."

"Any feds knocking about?"

"Hard to tell, those guys know how to blend," Hadji said. "Plus I'm their eyes and ears on this one. They're getting my feed."

"Anything else?"

"Yeah. Guido fixes his junk more than the New York fucking Yankees."

"You should be a reporter."

Seventy One

Choosing "The Strife is O'er" as the entrance processional at a Catholic funeral is a solid enough choice, with enough generic uplift and majesty to befit any of the bereaved, kind of a hymnal equivalent to a nice hotdish. Serviceable, sounds good on a big honking organ, reminds you what you're there for. Lacks the drama of, say, a Mozart requiem, but it gets it done just fine and no one's asking for their money back.

But to the million dollars' worth of suits and pinky rings in attendance, there was some notable mirth with regard to its selection. Contrary to popular belief, Guido, although no bibliophile, will read on occasion, especially when confined in situations not given to more traditional mafioso hijinks, not that it would be like snapping towels in a high school locker room or something. So, as several of the brethren pointed out the selection in the program—there seemed to be designated readers that were tasked with sharing with their neighbors, like orderly fifth graders in social studies class—there was *snickering*. And low-geared giggling, a special kind of mob laugh that had a devilish undertow, perhaps a laugh one might hear at a gentleman's club. Also a couple hand gestures that simulated pleasuring acts that typically weren't allowed in church. Sort of a nonverbal way of saying *you're fuckin' killin' me here.*

Damon also noted the irony of the aforementioned selection from the back pew, but didn't engage in any type of hand gestures or untoward language, spoken or otherwise. But he did have to engage the vibrating phone that was tickling his ribs, which was making him squirm and giggle. He flipped it open to see what it wanted. GO TO PICS. Add a flush of red. It was Kate Upton saying good morning. He put the phone back in his jacket pocket, only to have it tickle him again. HEH-HEH. SOMETHING UP WITH NEXT 2?

It was a black-and-white surveillance image of a man at the tabernacle, stage left of the altar, where the consecrated hosts and wine are kept for Holy Communion. His back was to the camera, but he appeared to be dressed in street clothes, all earth tones, oddly generic, so much so that it was like he was wearing camouflage. He blended in perfectly with his surroundings in the muted light. Phone buzzed again. AT SAME TIME. Damon called up the next picture. It was an old woman sprawled on the floor near the front of the church, by the parish office. She was being attended to by Father Guerrier and two other robed figures. Phone buzzed again. DIVERSION?

The heavenly warmth of neurotransmission.

He uses people like soccer moms and grocery clerks and garbagemen.

Or maybe some old lady scraping by on Social Security, willing to take a dive for a couple grand.

Pashtun.

That would explain half the equation. Damon trusted Hadji's gut reaction that it was a diversion. Initial reaction, first word, top of the list. Seldom wrong. Damon concurred. The fact that the guy was wearing street clothes took it out of the realm of possible coincidence. There are reverent protocols for any kind of attendance to the Blessed Sacrament. The priest isn't just walking up there in his khakis like he's checking the cereal cabinet in his kitchen. And the priest in this case was clearly accounted for, in his vestments, and in the opposite end of the church. Not accounted for was the FBI, and if they shared the same opinion. Damon texted Hadji: FBI GOT THIS? Hadji replied: NOT INTERESTED.

The second half of the equation not only found Damon alone, but was leading him into such a bizarre scenario that he needed a priest to see him through it. Although the theological guidance no doubt would be helpful, what he needed first was answers to basic questions that any Sunday school kid might ask. Then the questions would get harder. And weirder. Perhaps an odd request. And there was a clock ticking. Good thing he was in the back pew and Father Guerrier's office was right around the corner.

"Father Guerrier?" Damon tapped on his half-open door. "May I have a moment?"

"What can I do for you, Mr. Ramp?" Guerrier said, motioning him inside.

"Hopefully you can answer some of my questions." Damon took a seat. "Some of which might be kind of weird, so bear with me."

"Considering our first go-round, I would be disappointed if they were any less. Where we going this time?"

"Who gets served first during Communion at a funeral?" Damon asked. "I mean, is it the priest, the family—and does the priest eat the same Communion?"

Father Guerrier didn't respond at first. But there was a look. A really, really puzzled look. Damon got it—a guy with a really bad scratched up face was asking the Father who got the wafers first at a mob funeral. He also seemed worried that the priest was getting better stuff. Sure didn't see that one coming. He took a swing at it.

"Are you afraid we're going to run out?" It came with a bemused smirk. Touch of snark, too.

"No, no," Damon backpedaled. "Look, I'm being—"

Thunk.

At least it wasn't the gun.

Father Guerrier responded with another look. This one was an officious glance as he peered over his desk to the source of the *thunk*. The kind of look you'd get from a teacher when you were totally busted. The guy with the really bad scratched up face who was worried that they were going to run out of Communion wafers was also carrying a stapler. Actually, no longer carrying as it was on the floor. He hardly knew where to begin.

"You're better than the circus."

The ticking clock and the need to make up for lost time forced Damon's next move. He took the bold first step toward redemption. He pulled out his phone and called up the surveillance picture. He shoved it toward Father Guerrier.

"Know this guy?"

"No," Guerrier said. "Isn't that our altar?"

"It is. Remember when you were attending to the old lady this morning?"

"The lady who fainted?"

"She didn't faint. While she was on the floor this guy was doing something at your tabernacle. I believe he may have tampered with the Communion wafers or wine."

"Tampered?"

"I suspect poisoned," Damon said. "Back to my original question: Who gets served first? Keep in mind that the Naimo family are the targets."

"Oh. My—"

"Does the priest eat the same Communion? Because he goes first, right? Family might get tipped off if the priest drops first."

"The priest uses a larger host so the congregation can see it during the Eucharistic ceremony. So no, he doesn't."

"Family gets served first."

"Yes."

"Next one is the million dollar one," Damon said. "How do we stop it?"

"Oh my. Are you sure?"

"There's been at least a half dozen deaths in the last week surrounding this family. The two principals going at it are still alive, one of whom is sitting in the first pew of your church. All the pieces fit together like a jigsaw puzzle. Any ideas?"

The organ began playing.

"Where are we in the service?" Damon asked.

"That's 'I am the Bread of Life.'" Father Guerrier looked at Damon. The look was much different this time.

"Communion song?"

"Yes."

"How do we stop this?"

"Police? FBI?"

"Not interested."

Father Guerrier thought for a moment. Then his face lit up with a glint of an idea. "Ever see *The Graduate*?" he asked.

Damon ran the movie through his PC file for correlations.

"The scene in the church, when he's trying to stop Elaine's wedding."

"Yes—a *scene*." Father Guerrier looked at Damon until he felt satisfied that he understood exactly where he was going. "And you came up with this idea of your own volition."

"I have a gun and a stapler."

"A rollicking good start."

"And I'll need a hostage."

"Shoot."

Seventy Two

In addition to Damon lacking the punch to deliver a good blue streak, there was clearly insufficient menace to convince anyone, let alone a church full of wiseguys, that he was any kind of hostage taker. But never let it be said that Damon Aloicious Ramp wasn't a quick study. He instinctually knew that the sheer shock of the situation was going to carry the day. Some crackpot in a trench coat with a really bad scratched up face sticking a .357 in a priest's ear ought to do it.

"How we gonna do this?" Guerrier asked.

"Endgame is the most important. The Communion can't leave the chalice—I'll do it, you just need to point it out to me," he added, anticipating the priest's concern.

"The Ciborium. It's a chalice-shaped vessel with a lid, with a cross for a handle. And I'll still be aiding in the desecration of the Eucharist."

"That cow's already out of the barn," Damon said, suggesting that the desecration had already taken place. "Look, if we don't do this, a whole lot of people are going to die. And if you don't help me, I'm going to go all nuts on you with this stapler."

Damon tried on his hostage-taking face over his scratched up goalie-mask face. He removed his glasses, messed up his hair, and shook the gun around for some reason, trying to get a feel. He wondered what movie he got that from. Then he opened the cylinder on the gun and dumped the bullets out, pocketing them, just in case.

"Feel better?" Damon asked Father Guerrier.

"Well, at least I won't get shot. Your plan?"

"We're walking right down the aisle, you, me, a gun in your ear. Sound good?"

"You might need to explain yourself."

"Good point," Damon said. "How about *Freeze or the collar gets it.*"

"What, are you one of the Bowery Boys? Sounds like something Leo Gorcey might say."

"Shut up! Let's move."

"That's better."

"Thanks."

Curtain.

It wasn't the flashiest of entrances, but it sent the *Bizarre-o-Meter* up to ten. Up to eleven with bells if you were on the left side of the aisle, explained forthwith. To wit: A squinty guy in a trench coat with a really bad scratched up face and fright-night hair was coming down the aisle with a priest for a hostage, a gun in his ear. So far, so good. A helluva attention getter.

Just don't look too close.

The squint was hardly the steely-eyed glare à la the zen master of squint, Clint Eastwood. Damon's version was more Japanese sailor guy on *Gilligan's Island*, after Ginger took off his glasses, but a good corollary in that he had hostages, too. Also *good rooking*. Not so good rooking was the priest, who looked about as scared as a little boy staring at the bowl of peas at the dinner table. It should be noted that hostages should have a modicum of fear. An approaching toy poodle in a pink hoodie instills more fear than Father Guerrier was showing.

Now the forthwith.

To the congregants on the left side of the aisle, it looked like they were doing a really weird tango. They were missing the visual element of the gun, probably right up there near the top of key visual elements in suggesting a hostage situation. What was left was a guy in a trench coat and a priest doing a crooked slow-dance down the aisle at a funeral, which induced a degree of mirth among the residents of Guidoville. Also a couple of *what the fuck's*. There also was a *Hey look, it's the guy who ran into Sasquatch*. Pinky rings could be heard tapping on the backs of the pews. It should be noted that the congregation present consisted mainly of wiseguys. To them, this wasn't occasion to be alarmed. This was *the bleeping circus was in town*. The pinky ring taps signified approval. This was the most fun they ever had in church.

"This isn't working," Guerrier said.

"Keep moving, collar."

"Okay, Slip. We goin' to da candy store later?"

"A little more fear and a little less wiseacre, please."

"My wiener dog in a Halloween costume is more intimidating."

"Shut up or I'm putting the bullets back in."

Being of a precise nature and lover of clarity, Damon brought forth the explanation to the congregated.

"Nobody move!" Damon yelled.

"Oh, that was slick," Guerrier said.

"Or da priest gets it!" one of the Guidos said. Pinky ring approved.

"My bowels are movin' faster," another offered, to which someone else offered, "Eww."

Then came more Bowery Boys, Cagney and Bogart imitations, and some best-of from *The Godfather*. Guido loves a parade.

But the plan was working. Damon and Father Guerrier were at the foot of the altar. The look on the officiating priest was south of dumbfounded, but well on its way to florid. Maricella shared the same look, just got to florid much quicker. Antonio was his usual stoic self, but was having some difficulty maintaining it, a corner of his mouth turned slightly upward. Uncle Rigo had a look of perpetual befuddlement. He'd be hard-pressed to name his current planet.

Damon cut to the chase.

He let the priest go and charged up the altar steps. Then he paused. This was no time for a primer on liturgical vessels, of which there were several. He apologized to no one in particular, but sent his apology in a general upward direction.

Then he cleared the table.

Seventy Three

It was a gasp of such high magnitude that if there were oxygen masks, they would have dropped, only it would have taken a really long time because it was a church and had a really high ceiling. Then came a silence so profound that you could actually hear people thinking. And aside from the mesmerization of rappelling oxygen masks slowly descending from a vaulted church ceiling, they were basically all thinking the same thing:

Oh, *someone* is going *to get it.*

It goes by many names: *Perdition. Tophet. Sheol. Tartarus. Nergal. Enma.* Also Gehenna, not to be confused with Benihana, where you would find tasty teppanyaki instead of the destination of the wicked, the one in the valley of the son of Hinnom, not the one in Golden Valley. Symmetric perfection at 360°. It's *Gai Ben-Hinnom* in the Old Testament, and Grecian types know it as Yέενα. There are more names for it than you could shake a stick at. Incidentally, it's H-E-double hockey sticks in Warroad, Minnesota, Hockeytown, USA. It's—

HELLHELLHELLHELLHELLHELLHELL!

Purgatory. Hades. God's Penitentiary. If you were in Gotham City,

Chief O'Hara might exclaim, "The Devil you say!" HELL. On the way down you might hear "Runnin' with the Devil," "Sympathy for the Devil," and "Devil with a Blue Dress"—and in Hell, there is a special section dedicated as to whether it's *a* blue dress or *the* blue dress, from which there is no escape. HELL. Get past the Mason-Dixon and "The Devil Went Down to Georgia" pops up. Need to spruce up for your audience with the guy in the red cape? Ask for the "Devil's Haircut" at the barbershop. And if leather's your thing—and there are more leather shops in Hell than delis in New York—there's "Hell Bent for Leather" by Judas Priest. Can't go wrong with spiky black leather in the netherworld. And being a headbanger in Hell is like scoring a job with the federal government. HELL.

Damon Aloicious Ramp, meet Satan.

"Damon, for the love of Mike, what are you doing?" Maricella said, going with the M word instead of the G word, just to play it safe. Incidentally, *For the Love of Mike* was a 1927 movie directed by Frank Capra, originally titled *Hell's Kitchen*. HELL.

"It's poison! I tell you, it's poison!" Damon yelped, channeling a young George Bailey talking to Mr. Gower. Ahem. 360°.

Damon Aloicious Ramp was clearly on his way to Benihana. And if you're headin' south you might as well go in style. What came next assured him of a first-class upgrade. It also turned the gasps into sighing, head-shaking groans.

Damon was stomping around the altar like it was on fire, a probability so likely at this point that it had the congregation looking for flames and checking the fire exits. The officiating priest had gone from florid to on his knees, clenched in such a gripped fashion that it was unclear as to whether it was prayer or cardiac, but an opportunity nonetheless for a friendly wager among the bereaved—the line tipping toward a cardiac episode. Guido really liked this church. Throw out a buffet and this was better than Rat Pack era Las Vegas.

Maricella gave Damon another try.

"What do you mean, 'poisoned'?"

Damon gave one more stomp and blew out a breath. He put his hands on his hips and gave an affirmative shake of the head, a nod that said *that oughta do it.* He turned toward his sister.

"It was Pashtun," Damon said. "One of his men poisoned the Communion this morning. Hadji got it on surveillance. I didn't know what else to do."

"Really?" Guerrier chimed in. "Really? Was the stomping really necessary?"

Damon pointed at Father Guerrier. "It was all his idea."

"It was not!"

"Oh, c'mon, this is no time for modesty," Damon said. "It was a damned fine idea."

"Emphasis on the *damned* part."

"Roll of the dice," Damon said. This perked Guido up. Perhaps thinking a nice game of craps. Also got a *hmph* from the existentialist wing.

The officiating priest became officially incapacitated. He tipped over. The rustling of exchanging cash filled the church. Some of those special mob laughs, too. Guido's no welcher.

"Is it time for Communion?" Uncle Rigo said.

Maricella looked at Damon and shrugged.

"Guessing he's not going to help unravel our little mystery, is he?" Damon said.

"Got a plan B?" Maricella said.

"Think we're a little further down the alphabet," Damon said. "I'll get right on it after confession."

The somber tenor of the church service now sounded like casino night at the VFW hall.

"For Heaven's sake, people!" Guerrier shouted. "This is a church!"

"He dresses his wiener dog up for Halloween," Damon said, throwing over another accusatory point in the father's direction. Then he nodded toward the tipped-over priest. "Might want to check on your partner there."

"Oh, he faints like a woman in *Gone with the Wind*," Guerrier said. He nudged the stricken father a couple of times with his foot. "Father Cody? Father Cody, you okay?"

The priest started coming to. He looked around, wondering if he had it in him to get up for another round. Uncle Rigo was the first person he focused on.

"Are you going to do Communion now?"

Just like Scarlett O'Hara.

Sometimes it's better to just stay down.

Seventy Four

Damon slipped out of the church as nonchalantly as possible, his quiet extrication an attempt to right the funeral service back to its reverent moorings, padding off to the nearest exit, stage right of the altar. Although a literal and figurative step in the right direction, it was merely a step into a thousand mile journey, as the steps that came before it were about as quiet and reverent as Godzilla walking through Tokyo.

The aftermath was a close second.

The altar now resembled a smoking, debris-strewn stage after a heavy metal concert, complete with a passed-out dude, a guy in a coffin, and some space voyager waiting for splashdown. As for the smoke, it was basically a cloud of toxic carpet dust, as the carpet that just got stomped on looked like something that may have been installed around the Summer of Love, and probably was loaded with lead or cadmium, because there was a time when people thought that toxic chemicals just made stuff better. Probably was a toxicity quality-control manager back then, roaming the factory floor in a white lab coat. *Hmm...looks a little off—throw some more goddam lead in there.* The flotsam and jetsam were of a more reverent variety, a toss of liturgical vessels and linens versus plastic cups and underwear.

After giving Scarlett O'Hara another boot in the ribs that found him of little use, Father Guerrier went about tidying up the ship himself, a ship that looked like it may have tangled with the world's most popular atomic mutation on the open seas. In the middle of the liturgical jumble was a Swingline Model 767, which he slyly held up for Maricella to see. Then he pointed it at his head and circled it around a couple of times, to which Maricella could only shrug. Damned, maybe true, but a damn sight more entertaining than the circus.

The damned individual in question now found himself on the sidewalk, digging in like a ballplayer at the plate, scouring the soles of his loafers in effort to remove the mashed wafers that were now embedded in his shoes. Also finding him was Hadji, who could only shake his head and gesture with his hands in lieu of words, because there was a word bottleneck on the way to his mouth. Best bet is to keep it simple.

"You wacked-out freaking hillbilly!" Can't go wrong with one screaming straight across the bow. "Ya know, I—what's with the fucking stapler!"

"You know, if you can't say anything nice—"

"Oh my God. You have totally cracked up. Go see a doctor, you wacked-out freaking nutjob."

"Yeah, but other than that I'm pretty good, thanks," Damon said. "Get all that for posterity?"

"That was YouTube gold, Jethro. But we'll just keep it under the hat for now."

"You've grown so respectful."

"Yeah. WTF. And you've grown nuttier than a peanut factory."

Damon inspected the bottoms of his shoes to see how he was doing. Hadji took a peek, too. He really shouldn't have, because this whole thing was making him as nervous as a dove around Ozzy Oz-bourne. Somewhere along the line, Hadji picked up a little God-fearing, or something making him wary about tempting fate.

"Ya know, I usually don't go in for this sorta thing," Hadji said, waggling a nervous finger at Damon, "but you might want to look out for lightning bolts or the ground opening up and swallowing your ass, 'cause I think you just fucked with the universe or something. And that was a crazy-ass devil dance if I ever saw one. Even Moses slipped off his kicks before he threw one over them mountains, or something like that. Oh, shut up. *Wacko*."

"This really freaked you out, didn't it? I think we've uncovered a whole new layer of Hadji. Explain yourself."

"Kinda figure I got enough trouble, know what I mean?"

"Well, well, so there is a little guilt floating around in there after all," Damon said. "So go forth and sin no more, grasshopper?"

"No call for gettin' all crazy, Jethro. Guy's gotta earn, ya know." A little guilt, but it would pass.

A black crossover SUV with smoked windows pulled up across the street from Damon and Hadji. It looked brand new, as did the man in the black overcoat and homburg exiting the passenger side. But the voice carrying across the street was anything but, ringing a bell as distinct as Big Ben.

"Ah, Mr. Ramp, mighty wrestler of mean branches, and now God Almighty himself," Rumples said. He took Maricella's sartorial advice to heart. "Most unusual way of mourning you have. Now would be a good time for telling me what just happened. And don't hold back, I've still got mother's little helpers coursing through my system."

"Pashtun poisoned the Communion, of which you cared little at the time," Damon said. "I just made sure that the poison never reached its intended target, or targets, as it were. I don't think Pashtun was concerned with any collateral damage."

"Lab boys will get some samples. Damn curious delivery vehicle, don'tcha think? Think there's some political overtones in there, too, Mr. Ex-CIA Intelligence Analyst?"

"He's an operator, that's for sure," Damon said. "That was as diabolical as anything I've come across. Was there some statement in there as well? Sure, but it was secondary. Job One was and still is Antonio."

"Picked a helluva guy to cross up," Rumples said.

"Any leads?"

"He's a ghost," Rumples said. "Can be in plain sight one minute, then just disappear. And his pawns run the gamut from Sunni warriors to little old ladies. Where the hell do you start?"

"Jethro looks just like Antonio on camera," Hadji said. "Dapper him up, a little makeup, put him in the right place, be pretty good cheese for a trap."

A halo of lightbulbs lit up over Rumples head.

"Just throwin' it out there," Hadji added.

"Right over them mountains," Damon said.

"Put this wacko in immediate danger," Hadji said.

"We gotta get this guy, Mr. Ramp," Rumples said. "We need to put this one to bed once and for all. All necessary precautions will be taken. We'll have your back."

"Last time you said that I got kidnapped," Damon said.

"Brand new day."

"Maricella gets everything you know about her father," Damon said. "And I mean *everything*. If you're bullshitting, I'm sending Hadji back up to your farm to finish the job. Understood?"

"Understood."

"Then let's go fishin'."

Human bait. A very dangerous game.

Seventy Five

Ten thousand lakes got narrowed down to one in pretty short order. It was to be a fishing expedition of the urban variety, a slab of uptown asphalt as opposed to a woodsy fishing hole. The plans for this expedition weren't a whole lot more complicated than your average fishing trip, other than the fact that no water would be involved, and there was some identity confusion as to who was fishing whom. There also was a documented weapons cache out there, if one had an inclination to make a war of it. Other than that, pretty much a wash.

The cabal that gathered in Antonio's suite while the reception for his father was going on downstairs was well represented by both sides of the law. It was a mix of fed and mob guys allied for a purpose, sharing thoughts from their respective trades on how to take down a shared and formidable enemy. The deductive reasoning brought forth was decisive and on point, more street than scholarly, and free of masturbatory overthought. Damon enjoyed the exchange, as he always had believed that there was room at the intelligence table for all points of view, and found the inner-circle paradigm that ruled the roost as not only elitist but ineffectual. Inside politics always clouded the waters of policy. Street guys were unencumbered by the inside game, and went straight for the throat of the matter:

• Antonio was as marked a man as there ever was, and Pashtun would keep him in the crosshairs until he was gone. He already took two whacks at him, and a third was as sure to come as a sunrise—and it was coming soon, as that trigger finger now had some serious itch and twitch. Not enough to totally cloud his judgment, but an edge in making him susceptible to temptation.

• Taking a shot at the hotel would be too unwieldy and messy, would largely be a suicide mission, and the success rate of a head-on just wasn't there. A total Hail Mary. Not a hundred percent out of the question, but a good ninety-nine, and too ham-handed to suit Pashtun.

But at its essence, fishing is about temptation; the struggle of all flesh.

As old as the bible.

Even better when served up on a silver platter.

The platter in this case was of the wheeled variety and doubled as a very attractive bait. It was shiny, had a pretty color, and had a surprise inside, that surprise being one Damon Aloicious Ramp, playing stand-in for his brother Antonio, whom, not so surprisingly, took a pass on this one, but was nice enough to offer up his car. Didn't seem a whole lot concerned that his brother might get killed, but hey, you can borrow my car.

But it was a really nice car.

The Mercedes-Benz S-Class Maybach is not your garden variety wow-it-has-a-minibar rent-a-limo. What it lacked in cliché limousine kitsch was more than made up for by ineffably plush carpeting and enough white Nappa leather and burled walnut to appoint a New York penthouse. There was no rope lighting or tiny tree air fresheners to mask overindulged customers who insisted on making their mark, usually of an unpleasant variety. Rich also has a smell, and *good* doesn't adequately describe it. We are talking Frankenstein *gooood.* All told, a couple hundred grand's worth of shiny bait.

And like any good bait—plump, with a gooey center.

The aforementioned gooey element of this enterprise was being put into his candy-coated shell, the candy-coat not by way of Hershey but via the better-living-though-chemistry folks at DuPont. Playing the role of confectioner/valet in this case was Saverio, Antonio's closest personal security detail, and the shell being fitted as a waistcoat was a Kevlar vest. Saverio's job was to keep Antonio safe, and he was very good at it, having been doing it largely without incident for at least a dozen years. The largely-without-incident part meant that Saverio had been shot three times and stabbed twice. Even thicker than his scar tissue was his North Boston accent, an accent so thick that, at times, it didn't even sound like English. But Saverio was one of those guys who could get it done with very few words. The Secret Service for guys on the other side really knew how to get their hands dirty.

Filling out the rest of the roster as Antonio's security detail were federal agents, six in all, all outfitted in body armor, and all instructed to form an egg-shaped cordon around Damon when outside the car, a shell to Damon's yolk. Ground zero of this enterprise was Petal to the Metal, one of the Naimo family's operations, a choice chosen as best to flush Pashtun out, and given the chockful of nefarious goings-on there as of late, a check-on by the boss to see what's what had some solid plausibility. The plan was simple: Drive the shiny bait around the block a few times to register your presence and get Pashtun's juices flowing, then go away; casing and being careful add up to credence. Then do it again. This time stage it like you're getting ready to take the boss for a walk. All the patience adds plausibility, and you get an added bonus of extra time to put everyone in place—all hands, all over the place—to take care of business if opportunity arises.

Everything was in place but Damon's face. Since none of the cabal present was carrying any concealer, one of the maids was flagged down in the hall and pressed into service. Her ten minutes of emergency work netted her about three hundred bucks.

Close enough.

"Christ. He still looks like Gerry fuckin' Cheevahs," Saverio said, noting a resemblance to the famous goalie mask worn by the old Boston goaltender.

"Feel like I got his goalie gear on," Damon said.

"Nice. Keep ya head downna ya be fine."

An extra syllable or two is always reassuring.

Seventy Six

Temptation comes in all shapes and sizes. Curiosity being one, the perennial downfall of many a cat. Irresistible if you're a big ol' Chicago alley cat with a five-star smorgasbord beguiling you from downstairs.

While Damon was being trolled around the uptown area, Rumples thought a stroll downstairs might be entertaining, being as Guido conventions didn't happen quite as often as the National Grocers Association. There were plenty of good pickings to paw through, some hornet's nests to poke, and some interesting conversation to help pass the time, because no one regaled old war stories better than Guido, especially after a couple of Scotches to get the soldiers to charge. But first things first. Be a good guest and pay your respects. Then you can knock down the garbage cans.

"Miss Naimo, my sincerest condolences on your loss, I really mean that," Rumples said. "I'll try not to be too disruptive."

"Promise?" Maricella said. "Okay then. You can be a *little* disruptive, but don't go all nuts on me. Oh darn. Disruption in the midst. You have a gift."

There were some daggers being pointed at Rumples, all eyes for now, but dollars to doughnuts, some real daggers underneath to back up the glare.

Maricella called for a stand-down with a subtle hand gesture. Guido complied, consoling himself with more beef tenderloin medallions and portobello mushroom ravioli. Another Scotch wouldn't hurt.

"What's our current state of affairs?"

"Nice brother is standing in for not-nice brother, trying to flush out a lethal Afghan who's trying to put the lights out on the not-so-nice one," Rumples said.

"Nice. And where is my nice brother as we speak?"

"Uptown, doing some fishing."

"Sounds like he's on the wrong end of the pole, but I digress," Maricella said. "Of his own volition?"

"Yes."

"And the details of the deal?"

"I am to divulge absolutely everything I know about your father and your family."

"Thought we had that one after my cowgirl stint."

"Oh, a little sport, Miss Naimo," Rumples said.

"Kinda kicked all that shit for nothing."

"You came to the aid of a troubled Hereford in her time of need. I really am grateful, you know. Damage reports were a little discouraging, but how was I to know I was putting Satan's band back together again. That kid and that donkey went after that place like the Who in their destructive prime at a Holiday Inn. Good thing I didn't have a pool—it probably would have ended up with a tractor and a couple of TVs in it. I think they're still eighty-sixed from that place."

"Damon is a sweet brother—the other one's nothing but a well-dressed powder keg. How are you protecting him? He tends to get kidnapped around your operations."

"He's blanketed by a half dozen federal agents and there's platoon strength securing the area. Everyone's armored like tanks. We're just trying to flush out the bad guys and get a cease-fire before there's any more collateral. This thing's way too hot."

"Cooler heads tend not to prevail in my world," Maricella said.

Or in Damon's.

Between the body armor and the body heat of six federal agents—and a face full of makeup blanketing wounded skin that desperately needed to breathe—Damon was burning up. But the remedy of soothing cool that would break the fever would have a deleterious effect on the general state of his hide. Cool, though nice, meant a metaphysical step into the fire. Or line of fire. Either or any kind of fire at this point would be bad. Cool would be good. Fire, no good. Thanks, Frank. But sometimes a guy just needs to roam the countryside. Sure, there might be some pitchforks and torches, but hey, cost of doing business.

"Let's take a walk."

Seventy Seven

The decision to take a walk is generally not an arduous one. Most people are agreeable to the undertaking, as it is mostly pleasant and not hard to do. If you can stand, put one foot in front of the other, and have a reasonable surface to walk on, you're literally good to go. Add a pleasant backdrop such as a park, a woodsy trail, or a path by a lake or river, and you're in for one of life's simple pleasures. The synonymic verbs used to describe the incident of walking attest to its innate pleasantness; you can stroll, saunter, promenade, trek, traipse, amble, mosey, meander, poke along, roam, and skip if you're giddy. And, if you're feeling especially celebratory, *march* in a parade. Add a modifying adverb such as leisurely, cheerfully, brightly, happily, gleefully, sprightly, jauntily, or blithely, and, oh boy, you're surprised they don't charge money for this. There are those that use the term *constitutional*, but there are equal numbers opposed, as it seems to connote a different bodily function all together. And there is a synonymic term for the aforementioned latter, a term considered untoward in polite company, but applicable in that it was the first word that cropped up simultaneously in the minds of the six federal agents in charge of protecting the guy who said the word that started

this tortuous digressionary hop down the grammatical bunny trail.
Shit.

Damon Aloicious Ramp, grand poobah and guiding light of the Arduous Walk Society.

The airtight quiet of the car's cabin tensed, the vacuum filled with dampened radio communications and heavier respirations that ran parallel with the tension. The scratch and crinkling pop of Velcro and Kevlar being snugged ran with the nervous body movements, rustling unease against the leather. Weapons were checked. Positions of two-dozen-plus federal agents were readied and set. Everything locked and a go.

Time to hit the beach.

The right rear door swung open and boots started hitting the ground. Agents one through six, go go go, like paratroops leaving a plane. Landing was precise, each agent a piece of the cordon, tightening with each successive piece. The yolk of the egg came last, ducking into its shell. Ranks closed.

Boots on the ground.

The boots began to move. One hundred feet of buckled sidewalk from boulevard to front door, gangly limbs of bare oak and unkempt hedges providing zero cover. Twelve legs in hustling forward march, moving in unison over uneven ground, riding the dips and rises like a flock of birds hitting a thermal. One set of legs in inconsistent step with all of the above, but those guys at the top never know what the hell they're doing.

Thirty seconds in no-man's-land.

Though it was only half the battle—maybe even less than that, because no one knew what was waiting for them on the other side of the door—a collective sigh of relief was taken once the cordon was tucked safely inside. No pats on the back, just necessary exhalations needed for a quick turnaround and refocus. Everything needed to come down a couple ticks.

Aiding the descent was the atmosphere on approach to Tralfama-dore.

The slithering atmosphere inside Petal to the Metal crept like a prurient fog, an impurity of sweet smoke and iniquity wafting in spectral light, as though the DARK ROOM had devoured everything whole—like some venal Blob fattening up on defiled souls, thriving in the blooming, throbbing darkness. An appetite grown insatiable and unstoppable, the whole place needing to be frozen and dropped in the Arctic. Damon's senses lit up across the entire spectrum, his VU meters throttled full red. The agents were keyed on task, but the atmosphere was sucking them down like a riptide, each looking to the other for confirmation, looks that roughly translated to *what the fuck is this place?* The entire building was infected and spellbound, unstuck in space and time.

Then Milah came out from the back.

Or some facsimile of her.

What stepped out from behind the curtain was some kind of cross between Morticia Addams and Medusa, the ropy dreads slumping off her head giving her a list toward the Gorgon. Her face was bloodless and gaunt, every movement leaden, as though laboring through some kind of induced torpor; her once-sharp and bright eyes now dim and unfocused. She was a shell of her former self, under the influence of something so profound that it seemed her very soul was snatched away, captured by the voodoo of a Bokor sorcerer.

Or by the allure of a backroom stacked with heroin.

Milah didn't introduce herself or offer any kind of retail assistance, choosing to let a languid stare do the talking. It didn't say much, not that anyone was asking.

Well, maybe one.

Damon stepped out of the scrum of agents and moved toward her, testing for some kind of recognition. He removed his hat and put his glasses on to help things along.

He stepped closer, trying to center himself in her field of vision, which was slightly askew.

"Milah?"

There didn't seem to be enough of her left to offer any kind of response.

"Milah? It's Clarky, remember?" Damon said, hoping her pet name for him would trigger the recent memory. There seemed to be a hint of something in her eyes, as though her mind was connecting a neural thread. Damon sensed some kind of connection, and waited patiently for the words to come around the bend. They made it, but the journey had proved too much.

"What can I do for you, Mark?" she finally slurred out, the words seeming to swim, as though inordinately heavy. Known or unknown was anybody's guess.

While Damon was trying to connect with Milah, the agents had fanned out and searched the premises. They all returned to the main room, their findings conveyed via barely perceptible nods instead of spoken words. The agent in charge translated.

"Clear," he announced in a decisive bark, the definitive findings now officially delivered and final. He assessed a quick glance at Milah before turning his focus back to Damon. "Nobody home, sir."

Nobody home.

Seventy Eight

The mission was fruitless and the drive back to base was commensurately barren in its silence. It was successful in that everyone was making it back in one piece, but that was overshadowed by the simple fact that there still was one hell of a hot, dangerous mess lurking in those shadows, and lethal, ruthless, and clever running around in the dark was enough to give anyone pause. Reports were empty across the board. Once again, Pashtun had managed to give everyone the slip. This was nothing but an amusing little dog-and-pony show for him, if he showed any interest at all. He was showing up the feds and the mob as easily as a child's game of hide-and-seek. He was adroit at both, and that silence hanging in the air was knowing that the *seek* was still on.

Also still on was Reginald, manning his post at the valet lectern overlooking the half-moon drive of the hotel, resplendent in his scarlet vest, his welcoming smile in full bloom. There was a sprinkling of amusement in his countenance as he watched a seemingly endless line of federal agents single-file out of the Mercedes, like G-men wind-up toys in a Looney Tunes short. He had a polite nod for the agents, and their all-business manner and no eye contact warranted nothing more, and proportionately was more than they deserved.

Ever the consummate gentleman and peace-loving Rastafarian, Reginald kept ungracious thoughts to himself.

The smile was for Mr. Damon.

Not seeing Damon brought Reginald out from his post, and he leaned inside the ajar door of the limo to see what had become of his missing charge.

"Mr. Damon in need of assistance?" Reginald asked, extending his large hand in the offering. He studied the cabin of the Mercedes. "Irie, such fine automobile. Makes Reginald want to hitch ride! Round the park, James!"

The thought proved inspirational.

"I think you're onto something, my friend," Damon said. "Once or twice around the park might be just what the doctor ordered. Be a shame not to take advantage of this fine automobile, being as I'm already in it and all. How is Miss Maricella?"

"Miss M has such heavy heart. If only something I could do..."

"You are a prince, my friend, the way you take care of us."

"It is always my special pleasure, Mr. Damon. You and Miss M have brightened the walls of this grand hotel, despite many phone call! Hah-hah!"

Reginald was the only hotel staff who addressed Damon by name. He would forever be known as *phone call guy* to all the others. A few went with *scratched-up face guy.*

"Round the park then?" Reginald confirmed.

"Round the park it is."

Reginald closed the door and tapped the roof twice, and off they went.

The leather was pillowy soft and the cabin comfortably warm, a subtle warmth that enveloped ambiently, blanketing its fare in relaxation, fostered to an even higher level by a note of vanilla that emanated from the sheepskin, all commingling with expensive couture and the rarefied air that is the very essence of opulence, all probably toxic in one form or another, but heavenly just the same.

Damon had not issued directions or any particular destinations to the driver, it was as though he just knew what was right for every purpose, a true professional, silent and efficient. They headed east on Kellogg Boulevard and sneaked down to Shepard Road by the old post office, continuing east along the river, railroad tracks and sandstone bluffs to the left, the winding waters of the Mississippi to the right. It was a pleasant route, one Damon himself had taken many times before. If the driver took a right at the junction of Warner Road and Highway 61, he was beyond professional and anticipatory, and was approaching the psychic realm.

He took the right.

Damon straightened up in his seat.

There was no window or partition separating the cockpit from the passenger cabin, so words could be exchanged, if one wanted. Damon was seriously considering the *wanted* option, but chose to refrain for the moment, supplanting the *wanted* with the always-available and eager *rationalization*—the ultimate bench player for anything in life that doesn't seem to want to square. It was all really quite simple; the route the driver had chosen was simply a pleasant one, and that's all there was to it, nothing more, nothing less. Mere coincidence. A Sunday drive that thousands before him had taken, in wood-paneled station wagons full of bored kids to covered wagons full of kids who didn't know any better, and were probably just glad that they weren't stricken with typhus. *But if he takes a left at Lower Afton Road—*

He took the left.

Okay, one more time and the dial on the *Uncanny-o-Meter* flies off and hits Bigfoot in the ass.

He took the left at Battle Creek Road.

"Ouch," Bigfoot said.

Seventy Nine

And then he stopped.

Also stopping was *rationalization* in every possible shape and form, and all its toady little noun friends: *coincidence, happenstance, serendipity, luck, chance, fortuity*—and the stopping was only the half of it, because *where* he stopped was quite possibly where Bigfoot might throw a kegger for all his rowdy, hairy friends, or field dress puncture wounds from exploding imaginary scientific testing equipment that share the nomenclature of the old *o-Meter* suffix.

Also not a bad place to dump a body, which Damon was trying really hard not to think about.

The southern end of Battle Creek Road is an isolated wooded pocket on the eastern edge of town, where suburban development dried up in the 1970s, mostly due to its inhospitably hilly, ragged terrain. It is an unsettling anomaly of suburban real estate, its long, undeveloped nature giving it an almost haunted quality, made even more so by an abandoned housing effort that mysteriously never came to fruition, set back deep and alone off the desolate road, inviting the mythical imagination of a generation of suburban kids to turn the mole hill into a giant mystery mountain, a perfect nursery from whence urban legends are born. Nefarious motives were ascribed, and the myth-making had begun.

Being a man of curious nature and fervent imagination, Damon was familiar with the stories and the area's history, and it really wasn't helping. It was exacerbating an already fully engulfed, paranoid imagination, which manifested in a posture as rigid as the Empire State Building, topped with hair about to jump right through the crown of his jaunty homburg. Every *o-Meter* in inventory spontaneously *boinged*, and there was a run on field dressings at the Bigfoot drugstore. One more thing and he was going to go up like a Saturn V rocket.

Shiiiiing.

"You know, I really gotta stop doing these *one more thing* things," Damon said aloud to himself. "Because it never turns out well—I mean, when isn't there one more damn thing? And what the hell was that *sound*? Crap. I think I just did it again. Am I being kidnapped? 'Cause I'm pretty damn sick of that, too. Am I going up north again? It better not be another farm. How 'bout we mix it up and try somewhere nice? The Bahamas sound nice. Ooh, how 'bout the French or Italian Riviera? That would be delightful—and exactly who the crap *ARE YOU?*"

The driver didn't utter a word or offer a turn of the head. Not a glance in the rearview mirror.

But he answered Damon's second question nonetheless.

He didn't need a word.

It was the source of that sound.

Shiiiiing.

It was a knife.

A very long, very scary-looking knife.

And Damon knew exactly what kind of knife it was. Part of his intelligence work for the CIA had included an exhaustive overview on everything Afghanistan. From Alexander the Great to Genghis Khan; the Soviets to the Taliban; its curious penchant for kites; its wars and tribal culture.

Its bladed weaponry.

Which Damon suddenly, desperately needed to talk about. Fear had taken the oddest of detours, plunging underneath to the deepest recesses of his being.

Then it came back up.

It came back up like a volcano rumbling up to eruption. Pressure needed to build; momentum needed to gather. A bottom springboard was reached, and every anxiety, quirk, and fear vaulted toward the surface. And it was all burning on the way up, all systems spanged dead-red and firing all over the place, whirled in a strange hot loop. Damon was throbbing with fever; his wounds seemed to pulsate. The only relief he could think of short of a plunge in an ice bath was to open his mouth.

Like hitting a relief valve.

So he did.

"That sure is a handsome blade. A *pesh-kabz*, right? Recurved, full-tang blade, hooked butt, ivory or bone hilt. Designed to penetrate chain mail of seventeenth-century mounted and foot soldiers. Persian origin. Weapon of choice for finishing off those pesky British and colonial troops, back in the good old days. You had three go rounds with the Brits, didn't you? Worked pretty good on the Soviets and the Afghan army, too. You guys aren't much for taking prisoners, are you? I'm really hoping to be the exception here. Did you get that when you came of age? I know it's a ceremonial badge of adulthood for some Pashtun and Afghan hill tribes. I got a lousy merit badge for rubbing some sticks together. So glad it's not a sword—that's the *Salwar Yatagan*, right? Not that it makes much of a difference, since you got about a foot of blade up there anyway. Sure beats the bejeebers out of a Ginsu! Now the *choora* is more of a fighting dagger, favored by the Mahsud clan of the Pashtun Khyber tribe. Of course the Brits lumped them all together as *Khyber* knives, not that it mattered because you'd just lop their heads off at the drop of a hat anyway. Am I talking too much? Geez, I'm really burning up here—"

So he started with his hat and worked his way down.

Damon wrestled his tie loose and undid as many buttons as he could reach. In order to reach more, his suit coat and Kevlar vest needed to go. He wriggled out of both and got to some more buttons, then hastily grabbed his shirt collar with both hands and began flapping to get some cooling happening. He pushed his hair back and up, the pomade used to sleek up his look now working in the opposite direction, causing his hair to stand at full attention.

Damon was trying to cool himself with such haste that he hadn't noticed that he picked up an audience. Disbelieving, narrowed dark eyes—still, onyx stone eyes—were studying him from the rearview mirror, accompanied by a mouth commensurately agape in disbelief. His knife and menace had lowered in the process, leaving only the eyes and the uncertain shroud of motive. Damon was uncharacteristically inattentive to the subtleties happening up front, distracted by the sweeping rush of fever, which now had him flapping his half-buttoned shirt like a menopausal woman with a hot flash. Even the most devout of monks on a vow of silence would have had a word or two, because half-naked guys with really bad scratched up faces and fright-night hair about to take flight in the backseat of your stolen car are pretty hard to ignore, eternal damnation or no.

The man with the black eyes was no exception.

"You cannot be him," he began in a rigid English, a stiffened tone exacerbated by stunned disbelief, given the bizarrerie he had just witnessed. "You also have bad cat. Have most excellent solution for that."

The knife reappeared again, turning and glinting in the sun, the curved blade imprinted delicately with ornate flowery scales near the hilt, its shimmering detail mesmerizing Damon as it came into his view.

"The imprinting detail is beautiful," Damon said. "Such beauty wedded to such savagery. Such is the way of the world."

"Look like the innocent flower, but be the serpent under't."

"Macbeth."

The sound of sirens breached the distance, closing fast.

"The best laid plans..." Damon said. It was a breach in quoting protocol jumping from the Englishman to the Scot, and there was a brief chastisement inside Damon's orderly brain. Actually, two: one for the breach, and one for the anglicized substitution of *plans* for *schemes*, thus the Robert Burns quote was technically inaccurate. Inner-pedantic turmoil along with the lions and tigers and bears, oh my.

And it triggered a joke to boot, which he delivered like a drunk who could barely keep his eyes open:

"An Englishman, a Scotsman, and an Irishman walk into a bar," Damon began, now swimming in a thick delirium. "They each order a pint of Guinness. Just as they're about to take a drink, three flies land in each of their beers. The Englishman pushes his away in disgust; the Scotsman just fishes the fly out and begins drinking like nothing happened. But the Irishman, he picks out the fly and holds it over his beer. Then he starts yelling, "Spit it out, spit it out, you bastard!"

Hadji was right. Damon had finally cracked up. And he felt like he was on fire.

But he was somehow happy. He took a long relaxing breath, and finally let his eyes close in relief.

When he opened them, the man with the black eyes was gone.

Eighty

A nd somewhere along the way he had closed them again. Of considerable note was the duration of the most recent closing, as his most recent travel resulted in him being transported to a completely different time and place.

Damon opened his eyes to a bright new world with a most unpleasant smell, the latter being attended to by a light potpourri that was seriously getting its ass kicked. But there was another smell peeking around the corner, if only he could get around the damn salmon loaf. It was a much more pleasant smell, having a warm familiarity and softness, trying to rise above the malodorous fray. But it had a will and a wonderful way, and always knew just the right thing to say.

"Kidnappers are starting to take numbers to have a crack at you. And the Guinness people called—getting nabbed three times in a week is a new record."

Maricella.

"Hi, sister," Damon said. "Judging by the smell, I'm guessing hospital. How long?"

"You've been sleeping for almost two days. How do you feel?"

"How do I look?"

"You look like that dude in *Scanners*—right before his head explodes. *Wacko.*"

Hadji.

Up went Maricella's index finger. Class was in session again.

"You're slightly swollen," Maricella said. "Your cuts were infected. The doctor said it was sporotrichosis—it's called the rose gardener's disease. That was some nasty brush you cut through."

"Toldja ya needed to see a doctor," Hadji said. "Got in a good set though, before they knocked you out."

"What's he talking about?" Damon asked Maricella.

"You said some things," she said.

"What kind of things?"

"Crazy ass things!" Hadji said. "Way outer space shit, too, heh-heh. You were like channeling stuff—jokes, impressions, songs, had an adventure with Bigfoot."

"Complete with an honest-to-goodness dirty limerick. Warmed the cockles of my Irish soul. You are a card-and-a-half, Mr. Ramp."

Rumples.

"Here. You dropped this."

Father Guerrier, bearing gifts. Because you never know when you might need to get some stapling done.

"I'm keeping the gun in case you come back," he added.

"Hope I wasn't too much trouble," Damon said.

"Oh, you got trouble, mister," Guerrier said. "You need to talk to my boss about that—but not for another thirty or forty years. I'm sure you'll have built up quite a dossier by then. You'll be at the pearly gates longer than the Watergate hearings."

Damon gave himself some devil horns and aimed them at Hadji. Said some devily things.

"Knock it off, wacko!"

"Heh-heh."

"It was Pashtun, wasn't it?" Damon asked Rumples.

"We found the body of the limo driver by the flower shop," Rumples said. "But by then it was too late—you were out for a country drive with one of the most dangerous men in the world, who had every intention of punching your ticket. Yet here you are. How on God's green earth did you get out of that one?"

"I think I babbled like the proverbial brook. I must have talked him out of it. Then I heard the sirens. How did you find me?"

"Antonio's guy put a homer on your Kevlar," Rumples said.

"He's gone, isn't he?" Damon said, referring to Pashtun.

"Into the wind," Rumples said. "We had a perimeter set up inside ten minutes of him lighting out, and he still got through. He's a ghost."

"Who's going to haunt my brother for the rest of his life," Damon said.

"Literally," Rumples said.

"At least you'll get another crack at him," Damon said.

"Think I've had enough cracks for now. And I've got absolutely nothing to show for it. No drugs, no guns, no murderers. Oh for bleeping three, and the lot of it is still on the loose. I can't even scare up a lousy case of tax evasion. Plus, I've got a totaled government vehicle I've yet to explain. And then there's you three trying to knock down my house. Good thing I'm in a hospital—because I might have a goddamned stroke. Sorry, Father."

"They are a trying little crew," Guerrier said. "Perhaps you should turn them loose on this Pashtun fellow. They'll at least drive him nuts."

"This little demon alone has about four of my guys in counseling," Rumples said, pointing at Hadji.

"Boys still on their honeymoon?" Hadji said. He was always saying the nicest things.

"What about the prostitution and blackmail?" Damon asked.

"Little problem in trying to prosecute a federal blackmail case," Rumples explained. "Vics are all gung-ho for justice until they find out that the particulars they want to keep closeted need to come to light—which puts the kibosh on things pretty damn quick. We got nothing on the prostitution end; it's fallen under the jurisdiction of local law enforcement. I got a whole lot of nothing across the board."

"Tomorrow is another day?" Maricella said.

"Oh, eat another turnip, Scarlett," Rumples said.

"The sun will come out tomorrow?" Damon said.

"Put a sock in it, Annie."

"The future will be better tomorrow?" Guerrier said.

"You should have been president, Father Dan Quayle."

"Well, the world needs ditch diggers, too," a doctor chimed in from the doorway, waiting to make his entrance.

"And a belt of Dewar's couldn't hurt."

Eighty One

When it was deemed he was out of the woods from his adventure in the woods, Damon was liberated from the House of Badwhiff. He was rested, no longer in danger of scaring small children, and had a smorgasbord of pharmaceuticals coursing through his system to keep him from returning to the forest. He also had a nice schmear of unguent across his face, which made him want to stop at pancakes house, where perhaps one would find a nice smorgasbord, maybe even share a nosh with Gaear Grimsrud. Lucky for him his dining guest was Maricella, who was a little more loquacious than the sociopathic Swede. In fact, she was a downright geyser of information just waiting for some unsuspecting schlub to drop a quarter in. Lucky for her there was an unguented, unsuspecting schlub with some spare change holding up the other end of the log.

"Did our rumply friend have any enlightenment to share with regard to our situation, while I was out tiptoeing through the tulips?" Damon asked.

"Oh boy," Maricella said.

Damon was guessing that was an affirmative. Lucky for Maricella that the unguented schlub had enough change for a night at the casino. Also, when the light was just right, a nice sheen emanating off his face, which was sure to arouse the curiosity of some hoople-head before the maple syrup was put away.

"When faced with that kind of predicament, I always just pick a random spot and start. We can sift through the timeline as we go. So, fire at will, sister."

"Our father may not be your father, but your father might be the father who once was the assistant Father of the little French church, the Father whom my father killed and covered it up."

"Sale on *father's* today?"

"Are you okay with half sister?"

"I am okay with you regardless of anything," Damon said.

"If what Charles says is true, this all began with our mother having an affair with Father Monreale. Which, in and of itself, is taboo on so many levels. How it all started is unclear, but it seems the connecting thread between the two may have been as simple as our mother's family was from Monreale, as was the priest, and they must have met at some social occasion. There was a commonality, a chemistry, and an affair was born."

"As was the fury and jealously of her husband," Damon said.

"Of which my father had in spades. Giuseppe Naimo was a powerful, violent man. And as cavalier as Italian men are with re-gard to fidelity, you don't ever, *ever* mess with another guy's wife. And to make matters infinitely worse, Elisabetta became pregnant. But here's the million dollar wrinkle to this sordid tale: the truth of your paternity was never proven; there's an equal chance that either of them could have been your father. There were no blood tests, and obviously DNA testing wasn't available—only the reaction from a very vengeful, jealous man. The mere thought of even a chance of Father Monreale being your father was enough to put everything in motion, and ultimately, it seems, your banishment. That's why you never came back. You were tainted. Revenge was exacted before you were even born. Giuseppe killed the priest, and before anyone was the wiser, had the body repatriated back to Sicily. And he had the strings to make it all happen.

"But when the fury and jealously subsided there was the guilt—this was a man who killed a Catholic priest. And this is where the little French church comes in. The reason he chose the church for his funeral was that this was his self-imposed atonement. He was throwing himself at God's mercy, by returning to the scene of the crime."

"Kind of explains why he wanted to see me," Damon said. "This was a man who was squaring his affairs. I remember trying to read the look in his eyes, when we first met. There was so much being said there—such a profound longing and loss, it was palpable. And though he couldn't physically, I sensed he wanted to explain something to me. In hindsight, I think he wanted to explain *this*. Any clue as to how my stepparents were chosen?"

"The connection is unclear, but what you remember about being in the church as a child, with the mysterious man and exchange of some kind of package, may have been some type of furtive child support. I am sure you were provided for in some way. Could your stepmother be of any help with all this?"

"Oh boy."

"I would be curious to meet her."

"Umm..."

"Perhaps she could shed some light..."

Damon rearranged the syrups again. Straightened the salt and pepper shakers. Also the napkin sticking out of the dispenser, which wasn't quite square. Dusted something off his sleeve. If only he knew how to whistle, which would have paired nicely with his studying of the ceiling.

"Hmm," Maricella began. "Now I *really* want to meet her. Spill."

"She's old, she drinks, and she has a gun. She's also a little paranoid, which makes the drinking and gun part a little more dangerous. She was wearing a shoulder holster and talking like Dirty Harry last time I saw her. She's ready to go to war with the neighborhood gangbangers."

"And here I was thinking lavender, doilies, and a nice plate of cookies. What about your birth certificate?"

"That got fixed as well. My stepparents are listed as my parents. Giuseppe must have had some serious juice to make all this happen. I'm starting to see why Rumples was so dogged in pursuit of your family."

"And he's still got nothing," Maricella said. "To think of what he's been carrying around all these years, and not being able to make any of it stand is mind boggling. As big a pain in the ass he's been over the years, I feel for the man."

"I take it you're buying all this?"

"I couldn't believe it at first, but when I started to put the pieces together, everything fit into place. It explains a lot. How I knew my father—and all he was capable of—made it all the more plausible. Guess that makes me a believer."

"So all the kidnapping and volatility with the families around that time—and me being born in the eye of the hurricane—was just a logical red herring?"

"It appears so."

And as certain as March snow in Minnesota, a curious party appeared, to point out the unguented schlub. She was about five, plump full of pancakes, and seemed to have expected as much, as she was wearing pajamas, ready to sleep off her pancake stupor. But her giggling was soon stifled by an alarmed parent, who averted the cherub's gaze and whisked her back to their booth.

"That does it. I'm just going to the paper bag until I lose the Halloween mask."

"A nice secluded spot on the Gulf of Mexico sounds better," Maricella said. "We'll just park you under a palm tree until you're all better."

"Vacation?"

"Oh yeah. Any chance we could lose that thing grinding it outside our window first?" Maricella said, gesturing outside.

More hoopleheads appeared, cameras rolling. Management began to stir.

The gift that keeps on giving. He began to form letters with his arms.

V-A-C-A—

"I'm guessing no," Damon said. "He'll probably want to bring the donkey."

About the Author

PERRY ANTHONY was born in St. Paul, Minnesota and is a graduate of the University of St. Thomas, that saintly BA in journalism leading him down the straight and narrow to various writing adventures, including work for the Associated Press and a brief stint as a copywriter, where he wrote prom night themes. His second foray into fiction landed him in the pages of Iconoclast Magazine, where his first short story, "Tracing Flight," was published. Others followed, some of which not landing quite as well. *Hot State* is his first novel in the *Slightly Crooked Mystery* series. *Friendly Skies* will approach next, where more landings will be attempted, hopefully not requiring any type of flotation device.

CPSIA information can be obtained
at www.ICGtesting.com
Printed in the USA
LVHW030141121219
640224LV00015B/375/P